P9-CNI-629

Mango
Delight

To all the "dramanerds" who give it their all
just because they love it. —F. H.

STERLING CHILDREN'S BOOKS
New York

An Imprint of Sterling Publishing Co., Inc.
1166 Avenue of the Americas
New York, NY 10036

STERLING CHILDREN'S BOOKS and the distinctive
Sterling Children's Books logo are registered trademarks of
Sterling Publishing Co., Inc.

© 2017 by Fracaswell Hyman

All rights reserved. No part of this publication may be reproduced,
stored in a retrieval system, or transmitted in any form or
by any means (including electronic, mechanical, photocopying,
recording, or otherwise) without prior written permission from
the publisher.

ISBN 978-1-4549-2332-9

Distributed in Canada by Sterling Publishing Co., Inc.
C/o Canadian Manda Group, 664 Annette Street
Toronto, Ontario, Canada M6S 2C8
Distributed in the United Kingdom by GMC Distribution Services
Castle Place, 166 High Street, Lewes, East Sussex, England BN7 1XU
Distributed in Australia by NewSouth Books
45 Beach Street, Coogee, NSW 2034, Australia

For information about custom editions, special sales, and premium
and corporate purchases, please contact Sterling Special Sales at
800-805-5489 or specialsales@sterlingpublishing.com.

Manufactured in the United States of America

Lot #:
2 4 6 8 10 9 7 5 3 1
05/17

www.sterlingpublishing.com

Mango
Delight

BY FRACASWELL HYMAN

STERLING CHILDREN'S BOOKS
New York

R0448718196

CHAPTER 1

Name Shame

I t was an average school day. I arrived at my girl Brooklyn Minelli's house, rang the bell, and spent the usual five minutes waiting for her to finish chasing perfection and come outside so we could walk to school together.

Brook and I became friends by accident when we sat next to each other in homeroom on our first day of seventh grade. My family had just moved into the Trueheart Middle School District over the summer to be closer to my father's job. When the teacher took attendance and called out Brooklyn's name, I whispered that my mom was born and raised in Brooklyn, New York, and we just hit it off, especially when we discovered Brook's father owned the restaurant where Dada was chef. So our being friends was destiny.

When Brook finally met me at the front door, she asked, "Hey, Mango, how's my hair?"

I gave the same answer I gave every morning, "Perfect."

"Are you sure?"

"Positive."

Then we set off on our five-block walk to school, rehashing last night's phone conversation—which boy is the cutest; which teacher is the most boring or the most fun; a five-minute "would you rather" session (Would you rather eat a pizza topped with live worms, or shave your head?). Finally, we got around to our greatest passion: the Queen Bee, aka Beyoncé! Brook and I lived for the Beehive. *Did you see what Beyoncé wore in her new video, in concert, on the street, at a photo shoot, in a magazine, on the red carpet, matching with her adorable kids?* We were OBBB-sessed with Bey! I mean, who isn't?

Brook had long blond hair, and she was always trying to get it to look exactly like Beyoncé's. (Come to think of it, that's probably why she kept me waiting every morning.) My hair was nothing like Beyoncé's; it was just brown, and I wore it in a big Afro puff, easy-peasy. Even though I didn't look like Bey, Brook said I sang just like her, which was just totally cray-cray. I mean, yeah, I was always singing along to her songs, even the old Destiny's Child hits, and I knew every lyric and could copy all of her runs *exactly*. My parents gave me a Beyoncé concert DVD last Christmas, and I practically wore it out. I played it over and over, learning all her moves. I even pretended to be Beyoncé in the bathroom mirror, singing my favorite song, "Halo," while using my hairbrush as a microphone. The bathtub, shower curtain, toothbrushes, and shampoo bottles would fade away, and I'd be center stage in a stadium, fans all around me holding up their lighted phones, swaying as I sang the most beautiful ballad ever! LOL.

Anywho, as we arrived at school, we heard *tweet tweety tweet* and cringed. Brook and I looked behind us, and here they came: the Cell-belles, a super-clique of girls who thought they were better than everybody else just because they had cell phones. They constantly posted duck-face photos of themselves online and then immediately texted each other about it to get as many "likes" as possible, as fast as possible. They all had the same ringtone for text messages: *tweet tweety tweet*. I mean come on, how obnoxious is that? Brook rolled her eyes when she heard it and whispered, "*F* for originality."

The leader slash queen-diva of the Cell-belles, Hailey JoAnne Pinkey, glided up to us, flashed a fake smile, and said, "Good morning, girls."

I said, "Hi, Hailey Jo."

The fake smile evaporated faster than a drop of cold water on a hot griddle. I could feel my face morphing into a grimace emoji as she glared, sucking the life out of me like a Harry Potter dementor. "My name is Hailey Jo*anne*—not Hailey Jo, Betty Jo, Bobbie Jo, or Billie Jo. Got it, Tango, Mange-gro, Fango?"

I cleared my nettle-filled throat, "Sorry."

Brook stepped up, put her hand on my shoulder, and said, "Her name is Mango, by the way."

"Oh yeah . . . Mango Delight." Hailey Joanne revived her fake smile. "Like the dessert, right? Sounds delicious. Did your parents make you themselves or just order you off a menu?" The Cell-belles giggled and started texting each other furiously, even though they were standing right next to one another.

As their thumbs went into overdrive, I felt myself melting into a thin puddle of humiliation. Why did my parents do this to me? What were they thinking when they came up with this fruity name destined to torture their only daughter? *Mango Delight Fuller*! I mean, imagine how many ways kids could make fun of a name like mine.

"Hey, Tango All Night!"

"What's up, Mongo de Fright?"

"Man-Go From My Sight!"

"Hey, it's Strange-o Uptight!"

The pain goes on and on. Parents should think twice before they come up with names. We aren't babies forever. One day we're twelve years old, and there's lots of mean kids, bullies, and wannabe comedians who live to make fun of kids with names that stick out. If parents considered that, they'd be smart and give their babies normal, everyday names like Chloe, Khalia, or Brooklyn.

Tweet tweety tweet filled the air. The Cell-belles looked at their phones and covered their mouths, pretending to hide their laughter. One of them must have written something nasty about me, because Hailey Joanne turned to her and

4

crowed, "Oh no you didn't! I just can't, I just can't even. . . . OMGZ! You are the Queen of Mean!" With that, she turned and strutted into the school, waving her hand in the air like she was testifying in court. Her clique followed after her in a row like ducklings, copying her every move. Ugh!

Brooklyn flipped her hair and said, "Forget about Hateful Jo and her iPhonies. Mango Delight is a beautiful name, and they were just being mean because they think having a cell phone makes them better than everybody who doesn't have one. Like you. And me."

It was true; not having a phone did make you feel like a glitch in the eyes of the Terabytes. Brook and I shared the same miserable fate. Both our parents refused to let us have phones until we turn thirteen! My parents were worried about the bullying that happens on social media. *60 Minutes* did a story about it one Sunday, and Mom kept nodding along with the reporter saying, "See? See? This is what we're trying to protect you from."

Guess what, Mom, I thought, *You don't have to be on social media to get bullied. You can just stand in front of your school and get bullied for being polite.*

Both Brook and I had birthdays in the fall, so thirteen was months away. The months felt like years, because when you were in school, every day felt like a week and every week felt like a whole month. So here we were, both outcasts in a social media–obsessed world, sinking into the quicksand of digital irrelevance.

Brook flipped her hair and kept trying to find the bright side, "Actually, Mango, we're better off. My mother says kids who get phones too soon stunt their emotional growth. They replace their feelings with emojis. That's how come they're so mean and treat girls like you so bad."

"Girls like me?" I felt myself starting to melt again.

"I mean, nice girls like you. Like us. You know, we're not flashy like Hateful Jo with her bedazzled zebra-striped phone case. Always bragging about having her very own personal stylist, the best phone, the best clothes, and the best human-hair weave. I mean, please—all of that stuff and she still has a jaw like a pelican!"

I couldn't help myself; I laughed so hard, I snorted. When it came to throwing shade, Brooklyn was an eclipse.

"Seriously, I'll pay them back for you at track practice. I'm going to leave Hateful Jo choking on my dust. She will be dominated *and* humiliated. Real talk. Watch me."

Brook and I shared another obsession, Girls On Track, or GOT, as we called it. We met four times a week after school for an hour and a half of track training, running games, stretching, and sometimes just hanging out and having "girl talk" with Coach Kimble.

At the beginning of the school year, when Brook signed up for Girls On Track for extra-curriculars, I put my name on the list, too, so we could hang out more. We both grew to love GOT so much that we quickly moved up the ladder from "newly friends" to "friendly friends" to "besties," which is short for BFFs, but still means you're Best Friends Forever.

The bell rang. Brook patted me on the shoulder and flipped her hair, and we headed into the building. I didn't feel much better, but at least I was able to scrape myself up from the sidewalk. I wasn't a puddle anymore. And as I imagined Brook sailing across the finish line far ahead of Hateful Jo, a little smile began to tease the corners of my lips. The idea of my bestie grabbing the win to vindicate me. . . . OMGZ! Just the thought of it gave me life!

The day flew by. All I could think about was how Brook was going to avenge my honor at GOT practice. Hateful Jo and I didn't have any classes together. The only time we were together was at GOT practice. The mango pit—that gross feeling that grew in my belly when I was nervous, or when I was watching a scary movie or felt like something bad was about to happen—started to grow heavier as school ended and GOT practice began.

As we were about to enter the girl's locker room, my jaw clenched, and I trembled with a sudden chill. I stopped so suddenly that Brook slammed into my back.

"Hey! What the . . . ?"

"Sorry. I'm freaking out. What if they start laughing and texting about me again?"

"So, what if? Who cares about those iPhonies? We'll be the ones laughing when I humiliate the phoniest of them all on the track. Now you listen to me, Mango Delight Fuller. You can't let those bullies get to you. *'You're a survivor!'*"

Brook knew just how to get through to me: by using one of my favorite Destiny's Child songs. I took a deep breath and let Beyoncé, Kelly, and Michelle sing their courage into me.

Yeah, I *was* a survivor!

While we were warming up on the field, we heard *tweet tweety tweet*! Coach Kimble's hawkish eyes darted around all the girls stretching on the grass, "Whose phone was that?" The phone went *tweet tweety tweet* again, and everyone's eyes shifted to Hateful Jo. Coach Kimble walked over to her with her hand out, "Give it up. No phones allowed at practice."

Hateful Jo gave a deep sigh and held up her über phone, which she bragged had an app for everything. It was the newest, crispest model, and it could do practically everything but brush her teeth. As Coach Kimble snatched the bedazzled phone, it glistened so bright in the sun that I had to shield my eyes.

Hateful Jo said, "I only have my phone with me so I can listen to my Apps For Laps coach while I warm up."

Brook and I rolled our eyes at each other. We were so sick of hearing Hateful Jo go on and on about her training app and how, "it's like having my very own personal trainer in my ear pushing me to go faster and harder! Seriously, it's just so crisp!"

Brook called it "Apps For Saps," but deep down we both

wished we would hurry up and turn thirteen so we could have our very own personal coaches right in our ears.

Coach Kimble blew her whistle and said, "All right, ladies. Let's get on the blocks for the four hundred meter."

Brook said, "Want to hang out tonight?"

"Sure!" I responded. "Can you come over for dinner?"

"Mm-hm. I'll check with my mother." We headed for the starting blocks on the track.

I remember the first time I invited Brook to our apartment. It was just two weeks after we started GOT practice, and I was excited to show her Mom's old college track-and-field trophies, medals, and ribbons. Mom had been on the way to qualifying for the Olympics until she got in a horrible accident and lost her leg. I hadn't told anyone about Mom's false leg before Brook—not because I was ashamed or anything, but you really can't tell she has one because she always wears long pants; and anywho, since she never talked about it, why should I? But now that I had a true bestie and we ran track together and told each other everything, why not?

Brook always said I was born with natural track-and-field talent because of my mom. Still, Brook was a much better runner than me. Actually, Brook and Hateful Jo were the best runners at Trueheart. Brook despised the fact that Hateful Jo was just as good as she was. Their records were tied. Hateful Jo had won just as many sprints as Brook. They were guaranteed to come in first and second place. I was a third or fourth place kind of girl, but I didn't mind.

Running was fun for me. I did it for the rush that came when I got in the zone. It's like my whole body and even my brain floated way up high above the trees and I could see and feel everything around me, but at the same time, I felt a deep peace and happiness. I guess I got pretty Zen.

I set my feet on the blocks and placed my hands on the asphalt track. I looked over at Brook, who was two lanes over. We shared a quick smile, and I gave her a thumbs-up, happy knowing she was running this race for me. Hateful Jo rolled her eyes and shook her head, like she was saying "Give it up, loser." I looked away and focused on the track. I was not going to let her get in my head.

I'm a survivor. Just as I thought it, the song started playing in my head again. I could feel the beat. My muscles relaxed. I was ready to run!

Coach Kimble blew the whistle and we were off. The beat. The lyrics. Beyoncé's voice. The harmonies with Kelly and Michelle. They were all driving me, pushing me to run harder than I ever had before.

I felt like I was moving so fast, time couldn't catch up to me. I was so focused on the finish line that I didn't even peek to see if Brook was beating Hailey Jo. I powered through the finish, dipping my head just like Coach taught us. I felt great—loose and powerful. I finally turned my head to see if Brook won, when suddenly, Coach Kimble blew the whistle and pointed at me. Had I fouled? Did I take off too soon? Why was Coach pointing at me? I looked around; everyone was staring.

"Congratulations on your first victory, Fuller," Coach said, breaking the silence. "Looks like we have a new star on GOT!"

I had won the four-hundred-meter sprint. For the first time, I had come in first!

CHAPTER 2

Girls Off Track

I threw my fist in the air, leapt off the ground, and yelled. I turned to look for Brook, who I knew would be running to hug and congratulate me. But I was wrong; Brook was walking away. She swiped her towel off a bench and headed for the locker room. Weird to the extreme. I was about to run after her when Hateful Jo came up and gave me a high five.

"Good job, Mango," she said. "You were flying."

This surprising acknowledgment triggered the rest of the Cell-belles to do the same. I have to admit, the unexpected props and attention felt really, really good.

Brook was already dressed by the time I made it to the locker room, and things got really suspect on our walk home. Brook was unusually quiet. She limped on and off, saying she must have pulled her hamstring doing Frankenstein kicks during warm-up. That's why she hadn't run her best during the four hundred meter. It put a little ding in how great I felt about winning, but she was probably telling the truth. I mean, I had *never* beat her or Hailey Jo before. I explained about how I was hearing Destiny's Child's "Survivor" in my head while I was running, but Brook said, "Seriously, Mango, that's silly. Songs don't make you run faster. Hateful Jo and I were just having an off day, that's all."

I got quiet on the rest of the walk home. But that didn't stop me from noticing how Brook's limp would come and go as we made our way down the tree-lined streets of her neighborhood. I was going to make a joke about it but decided against it. I made a crack about Hateful Jo and her Apps For Saps coach, but Brook didn't even pretend to laugh or smile.

When we got to her house, I said, "I'll wait here while you ask your mom."

"Ask my mom what?"

"If you can come over and have dinner at my house?"

Brook kind of squinted at me, flipped her hair, and said, "Uhhhh . . . no, I can't. My leg. It really hurts. I might have to go get it checked out so . . . bye."

Brook and I had this silly hand-jive thing we do whenever we reach her house, which is eight long blocks before the apartment building I lived in. Our moves consist of four patty-cake claps, two snaps, a double shoulder bump, air kisses on each cheek, and a rib tickle on each other's left side. But that afternoon, Brook just turned abruptly and jogged to her front door, her limp and our hand-jive routine completely forgotten.

As I walked down Brook's block, which was shaded by huge Jacaranda trees, I began to wonder if I had done something wrong to make Brook act the way she had after practice. Could it be that my bestie was jealous just because I won one little race?

To get to my neighborhood, I had to cross Martin Luther King Boulevard, the widest, busiest street in town. It separated Brook's community, which only had single-family homes, from mine, where people lived in two-family brownstones or apartment buildings.

The trees on my block were scrawny, planted in dusty squares at the curb of the sidewalk and braced with sticks and wire to keep them upright. The one in front of my building was the scrawniest of all, probably because it was the first pit stop for all the dogs in our apartment building when they went for a walk.

As the elevator *galumphed* to a stop on my floor, groaning as the door slid into its pocket, I tried to shake the idea of Brook being jealous from my head. Brook was just having a bad day. Everybody has bad days, and everyone has the right to be cranky now and then. I mean—hello, I had my cranky days, too. I was sure that when I called Brook after my dinner and homework were finished, everything would be back to normal. On school nights, we'd always hang out on the phone watching our favorite TV shows together and gabbing for at least an hour or two. Imagining that I was to blame for Brook's bad mood was giving my little once-in-a-lifetime GOT win way too much credit.

Mom was in the middle of her *Muscle Torture* workout

when I walked into our apartment. She doesn't like to be interrupted when she's working out, but I couldn't resist.

"Mom, guess what?"

"What?" she gasped between sit-ups.

"I won the four-hundred-meter sprint this afternoon."

Mom stopped mid-sit-up and turned to look at me. "You won?"

"Yep!"

As surprised as she looked, I was even more surprised when she paused the exercise DVD and opened her arms to give me a hug. "Baby, I'm so proud of you! I told you that you were just as good as those other girls."

"Well, it was only once . . ."

"Don't give me that. You do it once, you can do it again. Start a trend. Believe and achieve!"

I laughed. She reached for the remote saying, "Let me get back to this before I cool down. Want to join me, champ?"

"No way. I don't know why you put yourself through this 'torture' anyway."

"I have to get back in shape."

"Dada says he likes you thicker." I said, giggling about the way Dada flirted with Mom when she refused an extra helping of rice and peas or dessert.

Mom blushed, "Oh please, I don't pay him no mind. If I don't get rid of this baby weight, my leg will never fit right again."

Right on cue, the toddler alarm came blasting on. Jasper,

my baby brother, was awake. Mom sighed and started to get up from the floor.

I stopped her, "Go on back to your torture; I'll get him." I spent the rest of the afternoon playing with the cuddliest, most fuzzy-wuzzy, Winnie the Pooh–looking baby brother on the planet. I took him for a long walk in his stroller while Mom did laundry. After dinner, I washed the dishes, did my homework—math, science, social studies—and read two chapters from my book about Anne Frank.

I had a report on Anne Frank due in a few weeks, and I was right on track with finishing the book. I even left myself enough time to write a first draft and a rewrite to polish it before handing it in.

About five minutes before our favorite sitcom, *Cupcakers*, came on, I dialed Brook's number and settled in for a nice long chat. Her mother, Mrs. Minelli, answered and said, "Brooklyn's not at home tonight. Her father drove her to the mall to do some shopping."

"Really? Brook didn't say anything to me about shopping with Mr. Minelli."

"Well . . . Brook*lyn*"—Mrs. Minelli really stressed her daughter's full name to let me know she disapproved of my chopping it in half—"doesn't tell everyone every little detail about her life or plans, and neither should you, Mango." Before I could apologize or even pretend it was nice speaking with her, Mrs. Minelli cut me off with a swift "I'll let Brook*lyn* know you called" and hung up.

16

By the next morning, I forgot all about the tension between Brook and me. It was a beautiful day, made even more gorgeous by the Jacarandas on Brook's street, which were in full bloom with their lavender flowers. When a breeze blew, the blossoms floated down from the trees. It was like walking through a lavender snowstorm.

When I walked up the path to Brook's door, I didn't even have time to ring the bell and wait the usual five minutes before she joined me. The door flew open immediately and Brook shouted, "Guess what? You'll never guess! But guess what?"

"What?" I squealed, because her excitement was like super-flu contagious.

Brook turned her back to me, reached into her pocket, and turned back around holding *it* in the palm of her hand. "Ta-da! I got a cell phone!"

And that was the beginning of the end of our forever friendship.

CHAPTER 3
Fornever

Walking to school, I felt as though I was having an out-of-body experience, floating way up high in the sky and observing myself back down on Earth, acting like the biggest phony in the history of phonydom. Brook was skipping and twirling and squealing on and on about her new phone, and I skipped and squealed and twirled right along with her. Anyone watching would have thought I'd been given a phone, too. Yes, I could be a pretty convincing fake when I put my mind to it.

Brook was breathless as she went on and on about how she managed to get a phone. "OMGZ, I was so surprised when my mother finally agreed with me that I should have a phone, too. I told her all about Hailey Joanne and her phone apps that help her run and warm up and cool down and all. And how I came in third in the race behind you and Hailey Joanne. That really showed Mother how unfair it is that I don't have the same *advantages* you two have."

"I don't have any *advantages*."

"Oh, you know what I mean. I mean, you really do. Your mom was a track star. So it's in your blood. And she must give you running tips and everything. Right?"

"Actually, she doesn't like talking about running much since—"

"Anyway," Brook broke in without letting me finish my thought. "My mother had a talk with my father, and he finally agreed that I needed a phone if I'm going to keep up with everyone else. I mean, it's only fair, right?"

I said "Right" even though I didn't mean it, and we both jumped up and down and twirled around together.

All of a sudden I heard that awful *tweet tweety tweet* sound. I turned around thinking Hateful Jo was right behind us, but she wasn't there. I looked to the left, to the right, up ahead, and I even looked up above into the trees, but no Hateful Jo. So when Brook held up her phone and read a text message from our super-enemy, I felt like I was being electrocuted, or at least what I imagined electrocution would feel like.

"OMGZ, Hailey Joanne wants me to hurry so I can show the rest of the Cell-belles my phone before classes start."

"Hateful Jo? Since when are you and—" Brooklyn cut me off mid-sentence again.

"I forgot to tell you. Before my father drove me to the mall last night, we stopped by the restaurant to, you know, make sure everything was running smoothly. I waved to your dad in the kitchen. Didn't he mention it?" I opened my mouth to answer her question, but Brook bulldozed ahead, "Annnnnyway, guess who was at a table finishing her dessert? Hailey Joanne! FYI, just to recap yesterday morning so you don't make the same mistake again, she despises being called Hailey Jo. She thinks it sounds immature and like a tomboy, which she certainly is not. So anyway, her father and my father got to talking, and my father told her father that we were going phone shopping. Hailey Joanne offered to go with us and help me pick out a really cool phone, and, well, the rest is Sis-story."

"*Sis-story*? Really?"

"Seriously, Mango, Hailey Joanne is a major coolsicle once you get to know her. She helped me pick out this bedazzled leopard-print phone case, which looks sooooo fabulous next to her bedazzled zebra-striped case. Then she showed me how all the gadgets on my phone work. And she helped me download the crispiest apps. The running apps, chat apps, emoji apps, fashion apps, selfie-filter apps, *and* music apps, too. We traded phone numbers and texted each other all the way home while my father was dropping her off."

"In the same car? You texted each other in the *same car*?"

Brooklyn gave her lips a rest, stopped walking, flipped her hair back, and looked at me with her eyes wide and head cocked to the side, "Uh . . . yeah. Duh. You'll understand when you get a phone, too. Now come on, the Cell-belles are waiting for us."

That two-letter word, *us*, was just the life preserver I

needed. For a moment, I thought I had lost my best friend—
that she had completely gone over to the dark side with the
rest of the iPhonies. But she remembered to include me; we
were still "us." I was beginning to become a little bit cheerier.
If Hateful Jo—I mean Hailey Jo—I mean Hailey Jo*anne* was
inviting Brooklyn into her crew, then she'd have to invite me,
too, phone or no phone. Brook and I were besties forever.

Unfortunately, it only took me three periods to realize
that forever didn't last as long as it used to.

Our first class of the day was language arts. It was one
of my favorites, because our teacher, Bob Levy, was so funny.
He was a huge guy; really tall and wide with a shock of red
hair that stood up on the top of his head like a cockatoo. Bob
was always doing strange characters and making weird faces
and beatbox sound effects. He was a human cartoon, so it was
hard to not pay attention in his class.

Bob also insisted we call him "Bob" which was extra crispy.
It made us feel like adults. Bob made the other teachers seem
like dinosaurs.

Bob thought he was destined to be a playwright on
Broadway. He was only teaching for a few years while he
was in his twenties. Bob and Mr. Ramsey, our music teacher,
collaborated on the yearly school musicals. The two of them
are total opposites. Mr. Ramsey was a small man—the
biggest things about him were his huge Afro and the goggle-
like eyeglasses he wore. Bob was always joking and making
the room laugh, as opposed to Mr. Ramsey, who was a little

tightly wound, nervous, and formal. We actually saw him jump at the sight of his own shadow once in the schoolyard. Still, word around the lockers was that the two of them worked magic together when it came to writing the annual musicals for our school.

This morning at the beginning of English class, Bob announced that on Thursday they would begin holding auditions for *Yo, Romeo!* the Levy & Ramsey musical retelling of Shakespeare's *Romeo and Juliet*. I never read that play, but I knew it was a tragedy about young lovers who died in the end. Brook leaned over and said, "You should audition."

I snorted, "Yeah, right!" As if I would ever be able to sing in front of the entire student body, or anybody for that matter. I cringed at the memory of the talent show the school held just before Christmas vacation. The kids in the audience were brutal. They booed a boy to silence when he sang "Silent Night" off-key; they laughed at the girl who did a stiff interpretive dance (she was about as flexible as a number two pencil); and, worst of all, the poor soul who did a crummy magic act got hit square in the forehead with a chocolate pudding cup (he actually licked the pudding off his fingers after wiping it from his face). There was no way I was going to open myself up to that kind of ridicule. Besides, the Dramanerds (that's what we called the kids who did any kind of theater stuff) rehearsed after school when they were preparing to put on a show, and I already had GOT after school four times a week, so it just wouldn't work out.

I was becoming a little paranoid because Brook had been so distant that morning in homeroom and in language arts. Her suggestion was the first time she had spoken to me since the bell rang. Was she trying to get me to audition so I'd drop out of GOT? Why would she do that? Just because I beat her in one measly race? I was no threat to her on the track. If I could turn back time, I would sing a slow Beyoncé song in my head and come in last place in that dumb race. That way my bestie wouldn't be freezing me out, she wouldn't have had an excuse to get a new phone, we'd have been cracking jokes about Hateful Jo on the way to school this morning, and everything would have been normal.

Brooklyn and I didn't have all the same classes. After language arts we went to math together, but Brook went to study hall and I went to an advanced-reading class with kids who read above their grade. Brooklyn didn't mind, because she didn't like to read books. She was way better than me in math, so it didn't bother her that I was in a higher-level reading group. I had my reading class just before lunch, and Brook always waited for me by our lockers so we could walk to the lunchroom together.

Today, she wasn't at the lockers. At first I thought she was late or had to go to the bathroom or something.

I'd been waiting almost ten minutes when the principal,

Ms. Lipschultz, came down the hall on one of her patrols and squinted at me. "Mango, shouldn't you be in the cafeteria now?"

My mouth suddenly went all sandpapery. Ms. Lipschultz had the coldest gray eyes on the planet. Even if she were being nice, her eyes were like hailstones, and they'd freeze you on the spot, whether she meant to or not. I pried my tongue from the roof of my mouth and said, "I'm just waiting for Brook, Ms. Lipschultz."

"I saw her in the cafeteria. She was already seated. Hurry up before lunch period is over."

I said "Yes, ma'am" the way Dada trained me and headed to the cafeteria. I felt heat rising on the back of my neck. Why had Brook left me standing there? Was it because of that stupid phone? If she thought having a phone suddenly made her better than me, then, well . . . she had another *think* coming.

I wasn't surprised as I entered the cafeteria and saw Brook at the Cell-belle's table with Hailey Jo—Jo*anne* and her crew. None of them were looking at each other. All eyes were in their laps, where they were keeping their phones out of sight. There was a no-cell-phone-use rule in school, but clever girls like Hailey Joanne and her crew would find ways around those rules—in the restrooms, locker room, in between bookshelves in the media center, or under the bleachers behind the gymnasium. The teachers weren't very strict about enforcing the rules against phone felons anyway, because they were always sneaking to check their phones, too. At the table, the girls' thumbs were busy blazing across their keyboards. Brook was laughing at something on her screen when she saw me and waved me over.

"Heeeeey, what took you so long?"

"I was waiting for you by the lockers," I said a little snootier than I intended.

"Sorry," Brook said. "I wanted to eat fast so I'd have time to hang out by the bleachers and mess around with my new phone."

Hailey Joanne lifted her pelican jaw and looked down her nose at me. "Don't get an attitude just because you still communicate with smoke signals."

All of her crew laughed, including Brook. I took a deep breath, hoping a real cutting response would snap into my head. I wanted to put her down, put her in her place, and remind Brook of how we felt about Hateful Jo. But the only thing that came out of my mouth was, "Whatever."

Hailey Joanne made the kind of frowning face adults make at toddlers who hurt themselves and are about to cry, "Aw, poor Mange-gro Sprite is Full-er-herself just because she finally won a race yesterday."

All of the Cell-belles howled, and no one was louder than their newest member, Brooklyn Minelli, my ex-bestie. I didn't want to cry in front of a table full of mean girls. I am definitely not the crying type. Boohooing now would be like throwing gasoline and a lit match on a pile of thirsty twigs, so I turned and ran out of the cafeteria. I know, *how dramatic*! But I couldn't help myself. I had to hide before my heart fell out of my chest and broke into a million pieces on the floor, which the mean girls, no doubt, would take pleasure in kicking all around the cafeteria.

I headed for the nurse's office to pretend I was sick and get a pass to go home. Unfortunately, as I turned a corner, I saw Ms. Lipschultz still on patrol, so I ducked into the girls' bathroom and hid in a stall.

I sat on the toilet, put my head between my legs, and took deep breaths. Even though I was all alone now, I still didn't want to cry. I'm not one of those super-emotional types who cries whenever the wind blows. Once Dada told me that Mom's sister, Aunt Zendaya, told him that Mom didn't even cry when she found out she'd have to lose her leg. I wanted to be like Mom: strong and dry-eyed no matter what. So I sucked in a deep breath and concentrated on my recipe for tuna salad, which Dada says is the best he's ever tasted. I use mayonnaise, Dijon mustard, boiled eggs, pickle relish, spring onions, chopped pimento, capers, and, of course, canned tuna in water. Then I add a dash of cayenne pepper (not enough to make it too spicy but just enough to give it a little kick) and a pinch or two of salt and pepper, and voilà, the best tuna salad in the world.

My eyes were still dry when I heard the door to the bathroom open. From under the stall door, I saw two pairs of shoes: pink patent leather with a low heel, and lime-green running shoes. I recognized the shoes immediately. It was Brook and Hailey Jo*anne*. I could hear the *click click* of their cell phones. They were texting.

I slowly and quietly lifted my feet onto the toilet seat. I would die if they knew I was in there trying not to cry. I held my breath, hoping neither of them would open the door to the stall, because I'd forgotten to slide the latch and lock it.

All of a sudden there was a huge burst of laughter, and Hailey Jo*anne* spurted, "OMGZ, Brooklyn Minelli, you are the new Queen of Mean! I have to bow down!"

Laughing, Brooklyn said, "No! You are. You're the queen!"

Just then the bathroom door flew open. One of the Cell-belles rushed in and shouted, "Lipschultz is right behind me!"

I heard two *thunks* and then quiet as Ms. Lipschultz entered.

"What are you girls up to? Are you using your phones in here?"

"I'm not," Hailey Joanne protested. "I don't even have my phone with me. You can check my backpack."

"I put mine in my locker so I wouldn't be tempted to look at it in class," Brooklyn added sweetly.

"Well, all right," Ms. Lipschultz said. "On your way. Now. Unless you need to use the facilities."

I watched the shoes of the three girls leave the bathroom, followed by Ms. Lipschultz's. I let my feet drop to the floor and hunched over. Had my bestie truly gone over to the dark side? Was she now proud of being cruel?

No, I thought to myself, that couldn't be true. I would just have to get Brook alone and talk some sense into her. She was a good person inside. A little thing like a phone—even though it was a big deal—couldn't have changed a girl so completely and so fast.

I left the stall, went to the sink, and turned on the faucet. I started filling the basin, planning to splash some cool water on my face, when I heard *tweet tweety tweet*. I looked around. I was the only one in the lavatory. Where had the sound come from? Then, *tweet tweety tweet* again. The alert was coming from the wastebasket.

Leaving the water running, I moved toward the wastebasket, lifted the lid, and there, lying amongst the pile of crumpled paper towels, were two bedazzled animal-print-cased cell phones. I reached in and picked up Brook's phone, the one with the leopard print. The screen was lit, having just received a text message that said,

H OMG! that was close!

I couldn't help myself. I knew it was wrong, but I used my finger to scroll and read some of Brook's earlier text messages.

H Mongo is jealous bc u have a phone and she doesn't. 😟

I know. 😟 B

H now that u've upgraded to a phone, u need to upgrade your friends. 😈

The sound of water filling the sink was drowned out by the bell. Lunch period was over. I could hear the noise of kids heading for class, but I couldn't move. My lungs were paralyzed. My best friend in the whole wide world had just done the most unforgivable thing ever. She'd made fun of my mother! Brooklyn Minelli really *was* the Queen of Mean!

My hands began to shake. I nearly jumped out of my skin when the bathroom door suddenly flew open, and that's how the phone slipped from my hands into the sink full of cold water.

Brook, standing at the door, screamed as we watched her brand-new phone drown.

CHAPTER 4

The Pressure Principal

Brook's blood-curdling scream brought the teachers on hallway duty flying to the girls' bathroom, where I was quickly apprehended and taken to the principal's office. After one of the teachers spoke in a low voice to Ms. Pegg, the principal's secretary, she looked at me over her glasses and said, "Have a seat, Margo. I'll have to call your parents in before you see Ms. Lipschultz."

"It's Mango."

She looked up from her computer. "What?"

"My name. It's Mango."

"Oh yes, right, beg pardon."

I sank down on the bench, the mango pit in my belly swelling to record size at the thought of my mom having to come to school to meet with Ol' Frosty Eyes. She would have to wake Jasper up from his afternoon nap, which made him really cranky. And this would interrupt her *Muscle Torture* workout schedule. . . . Oh man, she was going to be mad to the thousandth power.

The *tap tap tippity tap tap* rhythm of Ms. Pegg's typing made my eyelid's super heavy, and, well . . . I guess I fell asleep, because the next thing I knew, my father was shaking my shoulders, waking me up. I quickly wiped the slobber from the side of my mouth with the back of my hand and hoped I hadn't been snoring. Then my brain reloaded, and I realized it was Dada who came to get me. My mind started careening off into the über-dramatic part of my imagination. Why was Dada here instead of Mom? Did something happen to her? Did she misplace her leg? Or have a car accident? Or maybe something was wrong with the baby! Did Jasper's eczema get worse? Did he have to go back to the hospital? Or was he kidnapped, and Mom was out with the police searching for him?!

There is no way Dada would show up here if something weren't horribly wrong. You see, besides being the most handsome man on the planet, he was the chef at Minelli's Italian Restaurant, and he was always busy at this time of day making fresh pasta and prepping the kitchen for the dinner service. Something had to be really wrong if he'd left Minelli's to come all the way over to my school because of what I did.

He sat beside me, his almond-shaped eyes crinkled with concern, and said, "Mango, gal, *what a gwan?*" That meant "what's going on?" Dada was born and raised in Jamaica, and his accent swam all the way back to the island when he became emotional or worried or when he was hanging out with his Jamaican friends laughing and slamming dominos onto the kitchen table.

My throat was so swollen, I couldn't dredge up any words of explanation for Dada. He held me as my shoulders quaked and I drenched his shirt with tears and crying snot. I thought I would never be able to stop weeping until Ms. Lipschultz stepped out of her office. Her gray, hailstone eyes froze my tear ducts, and my crying jag was over.

Ms. Lipschultz directed Dada and me into the two wooden chairs that faced her desk. I thought these chairs were smaller on purpose, so she could tower over you from the high leather office chair behind her desk. Even Dada, who was a tall man, seemed shrunken facing her frosty eyes from his chair.

Although this was my first visit to the principal's office, it didn't mean I was a perfect angel who'd never been in trouble. My previous offenses were petty compared to what happened today. Talking in class. Passing notes. Chewing gum. Excessive giggling. Not obeying directions from staff or student hallway monitors (power-hungry mini-monsters who lived for the chance to carry a clipboard and push somebody around). They were the kind of violations your teacher would dole out punishments for, like staying after class for a private lecture; writing a two-page essay on "Sticking Gum

Under Your Chair and Other Ways of Spreading Germs to Your Fellow Students"; detention, where they kept you for forty-five minutes after school; or, worst of all, sending a note home to your parents that you had to return signed in the morning. But all of those "misdeeds" were piffles compared to the felony I was charged with today.

Ms. Lipschultz interlaced her fingers on the desk and got right to the point. "Destruction of property is a serious offense, Mango. Do you understand that?"

I couldn't lift my head to face her cold stare, so I just nodded and mumbled, "Yes, ma'am." A little part of me was hoping Dada had noticed that I was being polite, just the way he taught me. His lecturing me to say "yes, ma'am," "yes, sir," "please," "thank you," "you're very welcome," "I beg your pardon," and "excuse me, please" had not been in vain. I was hoping there was a slim possibility that my good manners would help excuse my crime in his eyes a teensy-weensy bit.

Ms. Lipschultz continued, "Then you must also understand that your actions come with consequences. Yes?"

I was beginning to feel like I was in court. Ms. Lipschultz was the judge, and I was the accused. I began to lift my head a little bit, thinking, *I can't be convicted without putting up a defense.* It was my right. I had learned that from watching *Judge Judy.* It was also my right to have an attorney represent me, but since I didn't have one of those, I had the right to defend myself. Thank you, *Law & Order* reruns.

I finally spoke. "I'm not guilty, Your Honor—I mean,

Your Principal, uh—I mean, Principal Lipschultz, ma'am." I cleared my throat and took a deep breath, trying hard not to keep sounding like an idiot.

Ms. Lipschultz sighed, "Brooklyn witnessed you tossing her brand-new phone into the sink."

I shot up out of my seat and thrust a finger into the air. "I object!" My outburst was so sudden and so forceful that I startled Ms. Lipschultz, Dada, and myself.

Dada patted my shoulder, "Calm down, Mango."

Ms. Lipschultz, having backed away from her desk at my outburst, rolled forward and said, "Take your seat, Mango. We are not in a courtroom. I'm more than willing to hear what you have to say on your own behalf. Just sit down and speak calmly."

I sat back in my low seat, unclenched my fist, and cleared my throat again. "Ahem! I didn't *toss* Brooklyn's phone in the sink. I dropped it. By accident. Because I was startled when she opened the door."

Dada asked, "Why did you have her phone in the first place?"

"Yes. Thank you, Mr. Fuller, that was my next question, too." Ms. Lipschultz said, cocking her head to one side and lifting her eyebrows in a "if you're so innocent, explain that, smarty-pants" expression.

Uh-oh. My inner girl-code alarm started beeping and vibrating. If I explained that Brook and Hailey Joanne had hidden their phones in the trash can just before Ms. Lipschultz caught them in the bathroom, I would be ratting out my best friend. But was she really my best friend anymore? My thoughts went back to what I had read on her screen—*she probably couldn't win a race with her peg-legged mother.*

Her peg-legged mother.

Her peg-legged mother.

Peg-leg—

"Mango."

I turned to face Dada. He said, "Answer the question."

My throat started filling with prickly nettles because of the pain I felt realizing that those words were texted by my best friend's thumbs. The only friend I trusted enough to bring into my home. The only one I trusted enough to open my mother's closet and reveal the trophies she had hidden away, because thinking of that part of her life was still too hurtful for her to talk about. Brooklyn was the only person outside my family that I was comfortable enough to share family business with and even sing in front of, and she *betrayed me*!

I lowered my head between my legs and tried to take deep breaths again, but it didn't work this time. The tears began to roll down my face and splash onto the floor. I was crying for my mother and mourning the loss of my bestie. I was all twisted up in knots, because even though Brooklyn had treated me so badly, I still couldn't rat her out. She'd get into trouble if I said what she was doing with her phone in the restroom and that she and Hailey Joanne had ditched them in the trash can before the principal caught them texting each other. On top of all of that, I'd be admitting that I'd been in the stall eavesdropping. And even worse, I'd be labeled a snitch for the rest of my days at Trueheart Middle School. Snitches are branded, scorned, and left to spend the rest of their school days in a social desert without water, companions, or even a compass to guide them back to society. As much as I wanted to put Brook on blast, the thought of being shunned for the rest of my middle-school life was too heavy to bear.

Dada rubbed my back. "Mango, baby, if you don't speak up for yourself, you're going to have to suffer the consequences of your actions. Honey, come on, try to tell us what happened."

I shook my head. It hurt too much to even stand up for myself.

Ms. Lipschultz leaned forward and spoke softly, "Mango, I understand that you and Brooklyn are close friends."

I shook my head again, unable to shout "No!" the way I wanted.

"I can see that something happened to cause a problem in your friendship, but whatever that was didn't give you the right to destroy her phone, even by accident. Perhaps you girls can work things out and become friends again."

This time, I forced myself to push past the nettles of pain in my throat and blurt, "No!"

"All right. That's between the two of you. My job, as your principal, is to rectify this problem as best I can."

My father spoke. "No worries, ma'am. We'll replace the phone right away."

"Thank you. Now, as for the consequences of your actions, Mango—for destruction of property on school grounds, I could suspend you, but I have never seen the sense in giving a child a vacation from school as punishment. Also, you're a good student, and I won't take away your ability to learn. However, because there is such a strong rift between you and Brooklyn, I am suspending you from Girls On Track for the rest of the school year."

I lifted my head and shouted through my tears, "No! I love Girls On Track. It's not fair." I turned to my father. "Dada, please!"

But Ms. Lipschultz continued, "We have plenty of other extracurricular activities for you to explore, but some distance from Brooklyn seems necessary. I also need you to apologize to Brooklyn. I think that should be handled here, in my office, when you give her a new phone. Do you agree, Mr. Fuller?"

"Yes, I believe that'll be best."

"No," I said. "I won't tell her I'm sorry. I won't make up with her. Ever!"

Dada turned toward me. "Mango, don't be disrespectful."

"I don't care. I'll never say sorry to her, not after what she did." Dada and the principal prodded and waited and prodded some more, but I wouldn't tell them what Brooklyn did. I wasn't protecting my ex-bestie; I felt I was protecting my mom. Protecting her from the humiliation of ever finding out that I had exposed her personal business and that, because of me, she was being ridiculed by the Queens of Mean.

In Dada's car, I couldn't stop sniffling and blowing my nose. I came to the realization that snot is a by-product of tears. The tear ducts must be attached to your nostrils somehow. Why else would your nose fill up with so much of that gunk when you cry?

Dada pulled into the parking lot of the mall and asked if I wanted to come in with him to purchase a new phone for Brooklyn. Looking down at my hands, which were holding the mess I'd made of Dada's bandanna, I shook my head and said, "No, sir. No, thank you. I'd rather wait here, please."

Dada reached over, took my chin gently in his fingers, and turned my face toward him. "Remember, my sweet Mango, sometimes when it seems things are falling apart, they are really just falling into place."

"What does that mean?"

"Think about it. Sit back, relax yourself, and let it roll around in your brain awhile."

I tried to take his advice, but I didn't get to do much thinking. It seems as though the minute I shut my eyes, I fell fast asleep. Crying and dealing with a bunch of emotions is exhausting. I didn't wake up until Dada had pulled into his parking space in the garage beneath our apartment building.

I knew my eyes were red and puffy from all the crying and

sleeping, so I was happy no one else was in the elevator as it tugged us up to the sixth floor. Not that I'm vain or anything. At least, I didn't think I was any more vain than any other twelve-year-old girl. Seriously, who wanted to be seen looking like they'd been through five rounds with a boxing kangaroo?

Jasper was in his high chair when we entered the kitchen. Oblivious to what had gone on, he started bouncing and holding out his chubby arms until I picked him up. He was happy to see me. It seemed he was the only one.

Mom, lips pressed tight together as if she were holding in a mouthful of scolding, only stared at me with her fists on her hips. Dada gave her a hug and placed the bag with Brooklyn's new phone in it on the counter. Mom immediately reached into the bag and took out the receipt. A hand went to her chest. "Four hundred and fifty dollars, Sid? Who buys a child a phone for four hundred and fifty dollars?"

Mom was the family accountant. She's the one who paid the bills, set the budget, clipped coupons, hunted for sales, and made sure nothing was wasted. It's not that she was a cheapskate, it's just that she felt responsible for making Dada's paycheck stretch as far as possible, especially since she stopped working when Jasper was born. It didn't make sense for her to go back to working full time until Jasper was old enough to go to school, because child care cost more than her pay as a manager at Target. She was a pretty good writer though, so she held on to her freelance job, writing articles on high school and college sports for the local newspaper. That job didn't pay much at all, but she hoped she could become the full-time sports editor when the current one retired, quit, got fired, or was abducted by aliens.

Mom took the box out of the bag and examined the phone. "This is top-of-the-line. What kid needs this much storage?"

"I know," Dada said. "I purchased that model as a way to sort of . . . make it up to Brooklyn for what happened today."

"You mean for what your daughter did," Mom said, looking at me and narrowing her eyes. It was always "your daughter" or "that daughter of yours" whenever I did anything to displease her. When her temper blasted off, she dropped me like a hot potato.

"What about what Brooklyn did?" I asked Dada, my lips trembling. "She didn't deserve to get a better phone for—" I cut myself off, not wanting to step into all of those emotions again.

Dada moved toward me with his arms outstretched. "What, Mango? Why won't you say what she did to make you destroy her property?" His brow furrowed over his almond eyes. I could see that Dada, the most easygoing man on the planet, was slowly losing his patience with me.

Jasper whined as I put him back in his high chair. "May I be excused, please?"

"No." Mom said, her fists back on her hips. "Not until we discuss your punishment."

"I've already been suspended from Girls On Track."

"I'm sorry to hear that, but that's the school's punishment. You also have to pay for what you've done to the family."

"What have I done to the family?" Unintentionally, my fists went to my hips, mirroring Mom and her attitude.

Dada held his hand up to me. "Watch your tone, Mango."

"I'm not being disrespectful." I dropped my hands to my sides. "But I think I should know what kind of horrible thing I've done to the family to deserve more punishment."

Mom folded her arms across her chest. "Your father just paid four hundred and fifty dollars to replace a phone you destroyed. Do you know where that money came from? Do you?"

I didn't speak, although I knew the answer.

"It came from the money he has been saving to open his own restaurant. To follow his dream. To make a better life for all of us. So your actions have cut into all of our futures. Do you understand?"

Dada held his hand up to Mom. "Settle down, Marjorie."

I pushed back. "That's not my fault. He didn't have to buy a four-hundred-dollar phone."

"Mango, you know Brook's father is my boss. If we don't make this right, it's not only you who is going to have a hard time. Do you understand?"

"I guess, but I'm still not sorry."

"Mango!" Mom said.

"I'm not!"

"Fine. If you won't be sorry for what you've done, maybe you'll be sorry for this: you will not get your own phone until you are *fourteen* years old. Not thirteen anymore but fourteen. Your actions have cost you another year."

"That's not fair!"

"Is it fair that you've cost your father nearly five hundred dollars? Is it fair that he has to walk on eggshells around his boss because of what you did? Tell me, Mango, what in all of this mess is fair?"

Jasper started to whimper, agitated by the raised voices and the tension that threatened to blow our kitchen to pieces. I wanted to shout at my mother, scream that it was all her fault. I didn't tell what really happened because I was standing up for *her*. I was hurting for *her*. Here I was protecting *her* feelings, and she turned out to be the cruelest one of all.

No one I knew had to wait until they were fourteen to get a phone. No one. Having to wait until I was thirteen when lots of kids were getting their first phones at eleven or twelve was bad enough, but if I had no phone until I was fourteen, I'd be more of a social outcast than anyone.

I turned to Dada, but he just shook his head and looked away. He wasn't going to go against Mom. They always stuck together, whether they agreed with each other or not. I wished I had a missile strong enough to break through their united front.

Dada broke the silence as he headed for the door. "I

have to get back to the restaurant before the dinner service begins."

Mom asked, "Aren't you going to take the phone with you?"

"No. The principal wants Mango to hand it over to Brooklyn in her office tomorrow and apologize."

I turned away. It would be a waste of breath telling them that I refused to apologize, so I didn't say anything. But I wasn't sorry for what happened. And although I was pretty good at pretending to be happy for someone when I really wasn't, I was terrible at faking my feelings to myself. I'd rather be banned from having a phone until I was one hundred and fourteen than apologize to Brooklyn—not after what she texted.

CHAPTER 5

Unsorry

Dada made cook-up rice for dinner before he left for work. It was one of my favorite meals. It had rice and peas cooked with coconut milk, carrots, onion, and whatever meat was left over from the week's meals cut into bite-size cubes. Tonight's dish had jerk chicken, pork, and ground beef. Cook-up rice was different each time but always a highlight of the week. Even so, I had no appetite.

Mom sat across the table from me, and neither one of us spoke except to ask to pass the orange juice or the soy sauce. Once in awhile, I would glance up and catch her looking at me. Her eyes were softer than they'd been a couple of hours earlier when she laid out my punishment. I sensed she wanted to make up with me, but my feelings were still way too sore to make eye contact long enough to give her an opening.

Dada always said, "My two best gals are twins in two ways: how beautiful they are, and how stubborn they are."

I loved my mother, but we did have lots of . . . disagreements. Whenever we reached an impasse—a point where each of us was deadlocked on our side of an argument—we settled it by saying "Let's agree to disagree." Then I'd walk away convinced I was right and she was too pigheaded to admit she was wrong. I'd bet a hundred dollars Mom felt the same.

After moving my dinner around the plate with my fork, now and then picking up cubes of spicy chicken, the meal was over. Mom took Jasper away for a bath, and I cleared the table and washed and put away the dishes.

I didn't have much homework seeing as I didn't finish out the entire school day, so I did my math assignment and sat down to read more about Anne Frank, who seemed to have similar problems when it came to relating to her mother. What was it about girls and mothers that made us so hard on each other? Well, actually, I wasn't hard on my mom; she was hard on me.

It was difficult to concentrate. Usually when I was reading, I'd get so wrapped up in the book that I'd lose track of time, but tonight was different. I was too caught up in how the day had gone so wrong to pay attention to my reading. I finally put the book down when there was a soft knock at my door.

I didn't even turn to look at the door, but I said "Come in" anyway.

Mom opened the door and asked if I wanted to say good night to Jasper before he went to sleep. I looked over my shoulder but not at her and said, "I'll be there in a few minutes."

I thought Mom would close my door and leave, but she came into the room. I could tell that her false leg was bothering her by the *step hesitate step* rhythm of her walk as she crossed to my bed and sat down.

"Mango, sweetie, I want to . . . well, to say I'm sorry that I was so angry this afternoon. I didn't mean to be the Wicked Witch, but things are . . ." I turned to face her, and Mom looked up at the ceiling for a second, almost as though she were trying to hold back tears. I turned away.

After taking a moment to compose herself, she went on. "Mango, look at me. Please."

I turned around in my swiveling desk chair. I treasured that chair because it swiveled three hundred and sixty degrees. Jasper loved when I would hold him in my lap and spin around and around. He laughed so hard one time that he spit up, and the force of the spinning chair whipped the vomit right into my face. Gross.

I looked at Mom sitting on my bed. Her head was down, but she looked up at me from under her brow.

"Mango, I know you are a good girl. The best daughter anyone could hope for. Truly. I know this. And because I know you, I also know that you couldn't, you *wouldn't* do anything as vindictive as ruining that child's phone on purpose. I know that even without your explaining what exactly happened."

My harsh feelings, like steel in the path of lava, were melting, and I guess she could tell, because Mom reached her hand out to me and beckoned. "Come." I got up from my chair and slid in close to her on the bed. Mom put an arm around me. "You and I are so much alike. Sometimes it causes lots of problems, but there are times, like now, when it helps me to understand how you feel." Mom looked deep into my eyes. "Apologizing is one thing that has always been hard for me to do. Very hard. Particularly when I knew the person I was supposed to say sorry to didn't really deserve an apology." Mom straightened out her leg and rubbed the stump a little before going on.

"When you were born, your granny Reva came all the way from Jamaica to help me take care of you. I was happy to have her here—at first. But, oh my goodness, after about six weeks, I would have rather climbed a tree in the rain forest and live up there with a baby, some cockatoos, monkeys, and who knows what other whoosey-whatsits rather than spend another moment in the house with that, um . . . 'challenging' woman."

I giggled, and wondered what bad word she wanted to use instead of *challenging*.

"I felt as though she picked on me all the time. Nothing I could do was right. I didn't hold you right. I didn't feed you right. I didn't sweep or mop the floor right. And my cooking— OMGZ, as you girls say—she lost ten pounds from refusing to eat anything I would set on the table. One day, she pushed me too far, complaining I was lazy and wasteful for using disposable diapers instead of the cloth ones that had to be washed and hung out to dry each time you pooped or peed.

Well . . ." Mom shook her head at the memory. "I snapped and told Miss Reva all about herself and how I wish she'd put her big bottom on her broom and fly back to Jamaica during the next thunderstorm."

My hand flew to my mouth. "You didn't!"

"Oh, yes, I did. Your granny locked herself in her room and didn't come out for two days. She wouldn't accept any food or water, not even from your father. I pretended to feel bad, but actually, it was nice to be on my own without that old hen pecking at me all the time. But after the second day, I realized that the one who was really suffering was your father. You see, he was in the middle. Torn between the two women he loved the most. So, I swallowed my pride, made a coconut cake from a box, took it to her door, and apologized. She accepted my apology but threw the cake in the trash without taking a bite." Mom and I laughed—that was Granny all right. "She took my hand, walked me straight into the kitchen and showed me how to make a coconut cake from scratch. And you know what?"

"What?"

"It was better than my box cake. Much better." I smiled and snuggled up to Mom. "Miss Reva and I spent the rest of her time here—another month—with her giving me cooking lessons *and* the space to take care of you the way I wanted. We parted friends. But most important of all was that your father didn't have to tiptoe around us anymore. Even if I didn't want to do it, I apologized to your granny for Sid's sake, because I knew that if the situation were reversed, he would have done it for me."

Mom and I put our arms around each other and hugged real tight. I understood what she was trying to tell me, and I spent the rest of the night awake in bed, trying to figure out what kind of peace offering I could make to Brooklyn, because remaining enemies with her could make things hard for Dada at work. I thought about making a coconut cake, but as much as I love Dada, it would have been too hard for me to resist smashing it on top of her head.

In the morning, I got out of bed before my alarm went off, sat at my desk, took out my stationery with the lavender paper and the big letter *M* monogrammed on top that Brooklyn had given me for Christmas, and wrote:

Dear Brooklyn,

I've been trying to understand what happened to our friendship. In just one day, we went from being besties to where we are now. To be honest, I've been jealous of you since we met to walk to school together yesterday.

My jealousy wasn't only about the phone, although to be perfectly honest, I was being a big phony when I acted like I was so happy for you. Now that you have a phone, we aren't equals anymore. You get to be a part of the iPhonies that we both despised so much.

It hurts that after all the time we spent with Hateful
Jo as our sworn enemy, she's now suddenly your best
friend after one night of shopping together. Where does
that leave me? Out in the cold, feeling alone and angry.

Still, what hurts most of all is the way you made fun of
my mother in your text. Yes, I know, I shouldn't have
read it. I know that was wrong. But I did read it, and the
things you said hurt more than anything has ever hurt
before. I felt betrayed by you, Brook, but I swear on my
little brother's life (and you know how much I love him)
that I did not drop your phone into the sink on purpose.
It slipped from my hand. It really did. I would never do
anything so mean or stupid on purpose because:

#1. I would get into terrible trouble, like I am now.

#2. I still care about you as a friend.

I wouldn't feel as bad as I do if what you texted had
been written by Hateful Jo, because you are my friend
and she is not. I hope we can move past what happened
yesterday and be friends again.

> Sincerely,
> Mango Delight Fuller

By the time my alarm went off, I was done. I scanned the letter once to make sure there were no glaring errors, put it in an envelope, licked it shut, and put it in my backpack before I changed my mind. I hurried into the shower, dressed, and had my breakfast. Before I left for school, I gift-wrapped Brooklyn's new phone. The apology letter would be my peace-offering cake, and the wrapping would be the frosting.

CHAPTER 6

The Cold War

I wasn't sure Brooklyn and I could ever be besties again. If we did patch things up, I knew our relationship wouldn't ever be exactly the same, but I had to try. I had to do my best to apologize, for me and especially for Dada. To make his life at work a little easier.

It was a nice, breezy, cool morning, the perfect spring day. As I approached Martin Luther King Boulevard, I decided to take a detour and not walk down Brooklyn's Jacaranda-shaded street. It would be über awkward if I ran into her coming out of her house. Principal Lipschultz's office would be a neutral ground where we could have peace talks and hopefully end the war with a friendly settlement.

Walking down the street adjacent to Brooklyn's block, I ran into Isabel "Izzy" Otero. She was one of my playdate friends in preschool and kindergarten, but since then we had gone to different elementary schools and lost touch. Now we were in the same middle school, and though we waved at each other and were friendly acquaintances, we never really took the time to become friend-friends again. I guess it was because I was so busy being besties with Brook.

Izzy called out to me as I passed her house. "Hey, Mango! Mango, wait up!" I paused while she ran, huffing and puffing, to catch up to me. I'd always liked Izzy. She was a chubby girl with the sweetest, round kewpie-doll face. And boy, could she talk! Even when we were in kindergarten, she would gab your head off. As she hurried down the path from her house toward me, it made me smile to remember how much that girl loved syrup. One day when we were little, Mom took Izzy and me to IHOP for lunch, and she ordered pancakes and drowned them in so much syrup that it was dripping off the plate. She actually ate her pancakes with a spoon, like it was soup!

"Oh my goodness! Phew! I gotta catch my breath. I don't get to run that much. Mamí says ladies aren't supposed to run. It's the boys who should run to catch up with the ladies. Ain't that crazy? She is always talking her crazy old-fashioned talk. Anyway, I guess I take her a little seriously, since I don't run as much as I should. And look at you! You be running all the time in that running club of yours. I don't know how you do it, girl." Izzy finally took a breath. "So what's good?"

"Oh, nothing much." I knew that if I got started on what was really going on with me, it would be around the school faster than a lice infestation. Not that Izzy was a gossip, it's just that a motormouth like hers needed fuel to keep pumping. So I threw out a diversion. "You look so cute today." It was true. Her skirt, sweater set, and leggings were always on trend. Since my mom was always counting coins, I didn't get the latest styles. She would only buy from the sale rack. She'd say, "It doesn't make sense to buy you expensive clothes, Mango. Every year you get taller and your feet get longer. We'd go broke keeping you in style."

Izzy said, "Thanks. I like what you have on, too. It's retro cool."

From any other girl, I would have taken that as throwing major shade, but I knew Izzy had a good heart and meant what she said in the best way. I smiled and said, "Really? Thanks."

"Totally. Studded jeans were so hot three years ago, I knew that style would come around again sooner or later."

She took a quick breath and went on, "Did you hear about my brother Enrique? He got accepted into Yale pre-med. That's right, he's going to be a doctor. Hashtag: I'm so proud. Hashtag: I'm so relieved."

"How come?"

"Because now that Mamí and Abuela have got their doctor in the family, the pressure is off me. I can concentrate on being a triple-threat superstar."

Izzy has always wanted to be a star. Even in kindergarten, when we did the winter concert lined up in our holiday best, singing "Jingle Bells," Izzy jumped out in front of everyone and started shimmying, shaking, and jingling as though she were the bells we were singing about. Of course, all of the rest of us watched as the rows of video cameras and camera phones swung in her direction while we were completely upstaged. You couldn't blame her though. Izzy just had an extra enthusiasm gene. She couldn't help always becoming the center of attention. It was in her DNA.

She was one of our school's leading Dramanerds. She was so good and funny, everyone looked forward to her coming on stage. Nobody ever booed Isabel Otero.

I had to go directly to the principal's office when we walked into school, but I didn't want Izzy to know what was up, so I stopped at the water fountain. "Okay, Izzy, see you later, girl." She waved as I bent down to get a drink, but before I could stand, Izzy was back whispering in my ear.

"Listen, I heard about what happened yesterday. And just so you know, I got your back. From kinder to the ender!" With that, she patted my shoulder twice and headed to her homeroom. I smiled. That was really nice of Izzy. Maybe we still had a bond. I guess I had been too busy hanging out with Brooklyn to notice.

Ms. Lipschultz's office was chillier than the freezer of an ice cream truck and not because the principal was wearing a gray suit to match her frosty gray eyes. It had everything to do with the way Brooklyn and I sat ramrod straight in the low chairs facing the imposing desk. Brooklyn hadn't even turned to glance at me when I entered the room. My chest felt like I was being hugged from behind by a grizzly bear. Shallow breaths were the best I could take while listening to Ms. Lipschultz lay down the law.

"Whatever happened between you girls is over now. I want no retaliation whatsoever. Do you understand?" I nodded, and I guess Brooklyn did, too, because Ms. Lipschultz went on. "Trust me, there will come a time when you both look back on this incident and laugh. It may not happen tomorrow or even next week, but I assure you, the time will come. Now, Brooklyn, Mango has something to give to you and something to say." She turned her frosty gaze to me. "Mango . . . ?"

For some reason, the low chairs just didn't feel appropriate for what I was about to do, so I stood. Surprisingly, Brooklyn stood up, too. We faced each other. The outlaw and the sheriff ready for a showdown at the O.K. Corral. I took a deep breath, "I'm sorry for what happened yesterday. I didn't mean to ruin your phone."

I reached into my backpack and took out her gift-wrapped replacement and the letter. I held one in each hand. "This is to make up for your other phone, and this is to explain what I was really feeling and to say how sorry I am."

Brooklyn took the gift-wrapped phone out of my right hand and ignored the letter in my left. She turned to Ms. Lipschultz and said, "May I go now?"

Ms. Lipschultz's eyebrows arched, dropping the temperature of the ice in her eyes to fifty degrees below freezing, "I believe Mango has written you a letter of apology, Brooklyn."

Brooklyn fake-smiled and said, "Oh. Yeah. Oopsie!"

Without looking at me once, she took the letter out of my hands with two fingers as if it were a tissue I had blown my nose with, turned back to the principal, and said, "May I go now? I don't want to be late for homeroom."

I could have sworn I saw frost on her breath as Ms. Lipschultz said, "You may go."

Brooklyn turned and left the room. My cheeks were hot. If I were a white girl, my face would have been as red as a traffic light. As I bent to pick up my backpack, Ms. Lipschultz said, "Give her time, Mango. I'm sure she'll come around." I nodded and headed out the door.

A part of me wondered if Brooklyn didn't look at me because she felt bad because of what she wrote about my mother and because she knew I really didn't throw her phone in the sink on purpose.

I decided I would give Brooklyn the benefit of the doubt— until something caught my eye in the wastebasket by the entrance to the general office. There, on top of a bunch of crumpled papers, was my lavender envelope, unopened, unread—*un*believable!

CHAPTER 7

Blindsided

A girl without a best friend is like a coat without a hanger. Lying alone at the bottom of the closet. Wishing it could be up above with the other clothes hanging around with one another.

The first weird thing about not having a best friend or a squad was where to sit in the lunchroom. Brooklyn sat with the Cell-belles and didn't want me anywhere near her now that she had replaced me with Hailey Joanne. I couldn't bear to sit with the GOT girls, because most of them were Cell-belles, too, and I wasn't on the team anymore. Izzy waved me over to share a table with the Dramanerds, but after one lunch period sitting with them and not getting their inside jokes or cracks about this or that Broadway show, I felt better sitting off by myself, sharing my lunch with Anne Frank, hidden up in her secret annex.

The second weird thing about not having a best friend or a squad was leaving school at the end of the day instead of staying for GOT practice. The campus was usually almost completely deserted by the time Brooklyn and I were headed home. Now, I walked alone behind other kids—kids who walk with their friends, talking, laughing, doing things kids with friends do. Maybe this was my fault, putting all my social eggs in one basket called Brooklyn. I hadn't called even one of my old friends from elementary school since I started at Trueheart. Maybe that's why I was so alone.

After school a few days later when I was bored out of my gourd, I put on my running shoes, grabbed my MP3 player. and went for a run in the park by my house. I stretched, did some Frankenstein kicks, high knees, and butt kicks, just the way Coach Kimble warmed us up at GOT practice. When I was finally limber, I started to run. Unfortunately, it wasn't the relaxing experience I thought it would be. My mind kept thinking about Brooklyn and GOT and how much I missed both even though I didn't want to. I tried to shake off those thoughts and concentrate on the music, but every song on my Beyoncé playlist brought back some memory connected to my ex-bestie. Finally, I tripped over a tree root and skinned my knee. That was it. Running was no fun while running away from things I didn't want to think about. I limped home, dabbed some witch hazel on my knee, and moped around for the rest of the afternoon.

My gloomy attitude spread across the dinner table like a fungus, so Mom suggested I try out for another after-school activity or club. Just because I was suspended from one didn't mean I was banned from all the others. I said I'd think about it, so Mom would stop trying to convince me she was right.

The next day it was raining really hard after school, so I decided to kill some time until it slacked off. I went to the bulletin board outside of the student council room and checked out the list of clubs:

Chess Club—nope. Chess gave me a headache, especially when I played someone who could beat me.

Book Club—even though I loved to read, they only met once a month. That wouldn't take up enough of my free time.

Cooking Club—Dada would like it if I did that, but I had tasted some of their food at bake sales and international food week, and I didn't think my stomach could take the abuse.

I went down the list: Sewing Circle, Computer Club, Soccer Maniacs, Gymnastic Fantastics, Bowling League, Hogwart's Muggles, Minecrafters—the list went on and on and none of them seemed to fit my personality or interest me enough to join. Also, I had to be very careful of what kind of commitment I made, because I knew that once I joined, I would have to stick with it. Mom would see to that. Even if I didn't like something I decided to try, Mom thought it was important for me to stick it out until the course or semester was over. That way I wouldn't become a wishy-washy hummingbird flitting from one flower to another.

After striking out at the club sign-up board, I headed to the girls' bathroom to make sure I wouldn't have to go partway through the long, rainy, lonely walk home, and there was Izzy, staring at herself in the mirror—crying. It was kind of awkward to walk in on someone just staring at herself in the mirror, boohooing. A part of me wanted to back out the door, but Izzy turned to me with a bright smile on her face and said, "Hey, Mango!"

"Hi," I said. "Are you all right?"

"Yeah. Girl, I'm fine."

"But . . . you're crying."

"Oh yeah, I know." She wiped her eyes. "I always cry before an audition; it helps warm up my throat and gives my voice a little emotional catch. It's a trick I learned from my *abuela*. She sang opera in Mexico before moving to this country with my *abuelo*. He tricked her into coming to the United States, you know. He pretended he was a doctor, but he really only shampooed dogs for a vet. But she loved him and knew he only lied because he thought she was the most beautiful woman he'd ever laid eyes on. So, you know, like my *abuela* says: if you can forgive anything in life, true love should be at the top of the list. But she says it in Spanish; it sounds way better that way. What are you doing now? I mean, after you use the bathroom. What's up?"

In the space of like ten seconds, I knew the history of how Izzy's family wound up in America, and now she wanted to know what I was doing. This girl shifted gears faster than a Ferrari. I took a breath and said, "Nothing. I don't have anything to do."

"Then come with me to the auditions."

"Auditions?"

"For *Yo, Romeo!*"

I backed away. "I'm not trying out for the show."

"So what? You can be my moral support. Everyone needs a moral supporter now and then. You know, just to give me a pat on the back so I'll feel brave when I get up to sing."

I had no interest in sitting through a bunch of *America's Got Talent* pop star wannabes howling their hearts out. Then I remembered the way Izzy whispered in my ear to give me courage before I had to apologize to Brooklyn, and I thought, *Why not?*

Izzy gabbed nonstop on the way to the auditorium, and I was grateful, because we passed Brooklyn at her locker, lacing up her track shoes. I didn't get why she was doing that since it was raining out and practice would probably be canceled . . . unless they were going to do strength training in the gymnasium, which she and I always found a way to get out of. It used to be fun coming up with excuses and then hanging out at DeMarco's eating pepperoni pizza until it was time to go home so we wouldn't have to tell our parents that we'd cut GOT.

Oh no, I was getting sucked into remembering the good times again. I had to stop it. Brook and I had avoided being at our side-by-side lockers at the same time since the phone drowning—or at least I had. Now, thanks to Izzy, I was able to pretend I was riveted by a story she was telling about how her grandfather groomed Idina Menzel's dog once backstage when she was on Broadway starring in *Wicked*. I didn't really know who Idina Menzel was, and I wasn't quite sure what *Wicked* was about, but I pretended it was the most interesting story I had ever heard to keep from looking in Brooklyn's direction. Even though Izzy and I weren't tight like that, I pretended we were. I didn't want Brooklyn to see how lonely and pathetic this coat on the floor with no hanger really was. Besides, Izzy was really nice, and I felt comfortable with her.

As we walked by, I felt Brooklyn staring at me. *Good*, I thought. *I'll give her the cold shoulder the way she gave it to me in the principal's office.* I was still steamed by how she had thrown my letter in the trash. How could we have ever been besties in the first place?

As we entered the auditorium, Braces Chloe was onstage singing. We didn't give her that name to make fun of her; everyone called her that because there were seven other girls named Chloe in the seventh grade. There was Braces Chloe, Biracial Chloe, Hipster Chloe, Basketball Chloe, Chloe C., Chloe H., and Boss Chloe, who got that name because she was the stage manager and leader of the Audio-Visual Squad, the group of kids in charge of everything technical that went on in the auditorium. She was also the coolest Chloe of them all because she dyed her hair blue and wore only blue clothes and had blue eyes. I guess we should have called her Blue Chloe, but she'd only been totally blue for a few months—too soon for a name change.

Braces Chloe wasn't half bad; her voice had a nice jazzy

quality. The room was buzzing with energy and excitement, but everyone was focused on Braces Chloe. The seats were about a quarter-filled with Dramanerds, most of who seemed to be rooting for each other.

The auditorium was huge, with about five hundred seats and a real stage with lights and everything. Izzy grabbed my hand and hurried down the center aisle to the first row. "Sit here. I'll be right back." She dropped her backpack in the seat next to me and hurried to sign in with Boss Chloe. I thought about thinking up an excuse to leave, but I was here for Izzy and didn't have anything to worry about since I wasn't auditioning. So I decided to sit back and be the best moral supporter that I could be.

My eyes were on the stage watching Braces Chloe end her song real jazzy-like when Izzy came back to our seats. As the room broke out in applause, Izzy leaned in and said into my ear, "What's *she* doing here?"

"Who?"

Izzy nodded in the direction of Boss Chloe—and who was signing up on the clipboard but Brooklyn. That was totally stray. The girl sings like a crow with a broken wing and strep throat. Why would she be signing up to audition for a musical? Not to mention she had GOT practice after school four days a week. As she handed the clipboard back to Boss Chloe, Brooklyn actually looked at me, smiled shyly, wiggled her fingers, and walked up the aisle.

"That's actually bizarre," I said as I joined in the applause for Braces Chloe. A part of me wanted to turn to Brooklyn and return her smile and wave. Maybe she wasn't so mad anymore. She probably realized she lucked out with the four hundred and fifty dollar phone Dada bought. We might be on the path to being friends again after all. Stranger things have happened. . . .

While a boy I didn't know was rapping or singing or performing some kind of mash-up of both, I was preoccupied, imagining scenarios where Brooklyn and I would make up and become friends again. I grinned at the thought of her going to Ms. Lipschultz's office, begging and pleading for her to let me back on the Girls On Track team. Ms. Lipschultz's eyeballs would thaw, she'd say yes, and Brook and I would go on to set a national record at the annual GOT 5K. Mom would write an article about us for the local newspaper, and the caption under our picture would read "FAST FRIENDS!"

I snapped out of my reverie when Boss Chloe called Izzy to the stage. Izzy leapt up from her seat before I could offer any moral support and ran to Mr. Ramsey at the piano with her sheet music. The piano started to vamp, and Izzy shimmied down to the front of the stage. She has a loud, deep, big voice and more confidence than KFC has chickens. Izzy sounded great, and her acting and moves had all the kids in the room laughing and applauding even before she was finished. I must admit, it felt good to be hanging around with the biggest star in the room. And Izzy was obviously right about crying before singing, because she sounded incredible.

A bunch of kids stood and cheered when she finished. I got up and joined them. She deserved the ovation.

Before we could sit down, Boss Chloe called out, "Mango Delight Fuller, you're up next!" I was so busy congratulating Izzy that I really wasn't paying attention, even though a part of my brain knew Boss Chloe had called my name.

She called again, "Mango. You're up. Take the stage." I was dumbfounded.

"But . . . but—"

Boss Chloe pointed to her clipboard and snapped, "You're next. Come on."

Panic-stricken with the mango pit growing in my stomach at warp speed, I looked to Izzy, "Did you . . . ?"

Izzy, her eyes popping out of her doll face, shook her head. Everyone in the auditorium had their eyes on me as I looked around the room. Then I spotted *them* in the back row— Brooklyn and Hateful Jo, their heads together, giggling.

My teacher, Bob, stood and said, "Mango, great to see you here. Come on, everyone's shy the first time, but we're good people. Go on up and do your best."

The biggest part of me wanted to run straight to the girls' bathroom and hide in a stall, but I knew that's just what my two enemies wanted. Yes, that's right: *enemies*. I knew it now, once and for all. Brooklyn was my sworn enemy. I wouldn't waste my imagination fantasizing about us ever being friends again. She did this on purpose to humiliate me. But I wasn't about to let her Queen of Mean plan come true.

Every personality trait has a good side and a not-so-good side. Yes, I was stubborn like my Mom, but sometimes being mule-like has its advantages. I raised an eyebrow at Brooklyn that said "You shouldn't test me, kid," and then strode up onto the stage like I owned it.

At the piano, Mr. Ramsey smiled, and that's when I realized I had no sheet music. Sweat began to form on my brow. I walked up to him and whispered my problem. He said, "That's all right. You can sing a cappella."

I shrugged. "But I don't know that song."

Everyone watching burst out laughing except Izzy. She dropped her face into her hands and sank down in her seat.

Mr. Ramsey corrected me. "A cappella is not a song. It means singing without music."

I said, "Oh. That's good since I don't have any . . . music." More laughter. I felt as though I would just spontaneously combust right there on stage, leaving only a pile of embarrassed ashes.

Mr. Ramsey said quietly, "What song do you know the words to?" The only song I could think of right at that second was "Halo" by Beyoncé. I told him and he said, "A Beyoncé song? Uh . . . that's kind of a rangy. Pretty difficult for most singers."

I didn't think it was so hard. I mean, I'd sung it a hundred times in my bathroom. And of course, Mom and I watched my concert DVD a million times. I looked over to Mr. Ramsey and said, "That's what I'd like to sing."

He nodded and said, "Okay, I can probably fake it and play along with some chords. What key?"

Key? Hmm . . . I didn't want to make a fool of myself again, so I thought for a minute just to make sure he wasn't asking me about my house keys. I said, "The Beyoncé key." His eyebrows rose to meet his hairline, but he shrugged and began playing a few opening chords.

I turned toward the kids in the seats. I noticed that Brooklyn and Hateful Jo, the Queens of Mean, were holding up their cell phones to video record me. I closed my eyes to block them out. I was not going to let them win. "Halo" was a song about love and feeling love all around you. That's what I willed myself to feel. I was too stubborn to let those mean girls make a fool of me. Marjorie Fuller's daughter was nobody's punk!

I closed my eyes and imagined myself back in my bathroom, and then pictured it transforming into a stadium, like I always did. A million people raised their lighted cell phones, swaying along with me. I was lifted by the chords from the piano, the lyrics I was about to sing, and the Queen Bee in me.

I started to sing. I lifted my hand like I was holding my hairbrush/microphone. My body began to sway to the music. The shyness I felt about singing in public fell away completely, and I just let the music and lyrics take me over. Suddenly, I was brave enough to reach for the highest notes, and I hit them with ease. Something inside me must have been waiting for this moment all my life, because I sang a few runs that I had never even tried before. My voice felt stronger than it ever had, and I belted out the last note to the end of my breath.

When I was done, I let the stadium in my mind disappear, and I was back at school. I could hear the lights above the stage buzzing. Somewhere in the hallway, a locker door slammed. My body was vibrating, as though every pore on my skin was charged with electricity. Finally, I opened my eyes and looked out into the rows of kids in the auditorium.

That was the moment the room exploded.

Kids were jumping up and down and standing on their seats. Bob, sitting in the front row with a notepad on his lap, just stared at me with a hand on his forehead as if he were checking to see if he had a fever. I was tackled by Izzy, who had rushed onto the stage to hug me. She had tears in her eyes, and so did Mr. Ramsey, sitting at the piano.

I didn't think to look and see how Brooklyn and Hailey Joanne reacted. I couldn't be bothered with anything negative. Not now. In this moment, the mean girls did not exist anymore. I had sung in front of a bunch of people for the first time in my life. *Good, great, fantastic, amazing*—all of those words were too small to describe the feeling running through my mind and body.

I was feeling something I had never felt before, a feeling I think I could call absolute triumph.

CHAPTER 8

What Goes Up . . .

I zzy never took one breath on the walk home. She went on and on about how great my audition was and how I would most likely be cast as one of the leading parts in the show. Although my feet were still floating a foot off the ground, I kept shaking my head. I never meant to audition in the first place, I was set up by a dirty trick played by my EFF (Ex-Friend Forever), Brooklyn.

Besides, maybe it's true that I could sing, but I was no actor. Never thought about it. Never wanted to be an actor. I really liked running, and my plan since starting GOT was to continue my mom's legacy from where she left off—trying to qualify for the Olympics. And when my running days were over, I would become a sports reporter—not working freelance for a newspaper like Mom but on TV with ESPN or some other sports network. I figured I could be myself in front of a camera, talking about something I loved. But playing a part? Learning lines? Dancing? There was no way I could do any of those things. And most important of all, I didn't want to.

"Are you kidding? Seriously, Mango, you've got talent, and that should never go to waste. Don't tell me you weren't ecstatic when everybody was cheering, jumping on chairs, and whistling for you. Bob looked like his head was going to explode."

"Okay, I admit it," I said, my face getting all hot again. "It did feel amazing, but—"

Izzy stuck out her rear end and pointed to it. "*Butt* is what you sit on; *talent* is what you bank on." I laughed as she went on and on. "You've got a golden throat, girl. Quit hiding your light! Step up to the plate and swing for the stars." Izzy got all dramatic and mimed holding a bat over the plate, waiting for the pitch, and hitting a home run without an ounce of self-consciousness. I was über impressed. Gotta love a crazy kid like that.

I said what I usually said to Mom when I wanted her to drop the subject: "I'll think about it. I will. I promise."

My tactic didn't work on Izzy, because when we arrived at her house, she took both my hands in hers and squeezed them really tight. "Mango, there ain't nothing to think about. You may not know it yet, but you need to put a big red circle around today's date on your calendar, because you'll want to remember this as the day you found your destiny. Did I ever tell you about my *tía*, Maria Magdelena? She was a psychic with a gambling addiction who died in a car crash that she predicted right before she drove off to pay her bookie."

I shook my head, sure that I would have remembered hearing about her.

"Anyway, she used to tell me, 'Isabel, one day you'll be struck by the lightning bolt of fate and *bang*! You will know your destiny. Pay attention to that lightning bolt. Follow it to the end of the rainbow, or for the rest of your life, your pockets will be so full of regret that there'll be no room for money.'" Izzy squeezed my hands even tighter. "You get it? You understand what I'm saying?"

I pried my hands away before she cut off my circulation. "Yes. Yes, I get it."

"Good. Don't forget to take a super-hot steamy shower before bed. Keeps the vocal cords ready to rock. Girl, we are going to have so much fun being in a show together. Just like when we were back in kindergarten." She turned and headed up her walkway, singing at the top of her lungs, "*Haloooooo ooh-ooh*!!"

As I walked the long blocks home, I thought about Izzy's aunt, Maria Magdelena. If she really was psychic, why did she lose all of her money gambling? And if she predicted her death in the car crash, why did she get in the car? How good could her predictions be if she couldn't save her money or her life?

This afternoon had been like a dream. Actually, it had been more like nightmare that took a sharp left on Luck Street and turned out incredible. I decided it was foolish to waste my time worrying about getting a part in the play. Bob knew how inexperienced I was—I didn't even know a cappella wasn't a song. Still, maybe it wouldn't be so bad to be in the chorus. That way I could just hang out and sing along with a bunch of kids. And if I had to do a little bit of dancing, I'd make sure they put me in the back, so I could copy the steps of the dancers in front of me and definitely not be the center of attention.

Another good thing was that I'd have something to do after school for the rest of the semester, and maybe I could make some new friends. True, I would be called a Dramanerd behind my back, but that didn't really matter. Look at how nice they'd all been this afternoon. I'd rather hang out with nerds that were kind than with jocks that hated on me.

When I got upstairs to our apartment, Mom was already in the living room, huffing and puffing to her *Muscle Torture* DVD. I was so anxious to tell my family about what had happened this afternoon. I was like a bottle of soda that had been shaken before it was opened; excitement was fizzing inside of me. But the TV was so loud and Mom was so busy sweating that I decided I'd take Jasper to the playground first and tell her all about it later, after she had toweled off. I went into Mom's bedroom to see if Jasper was awake in his crib, but he wasn't there. That was strange. He was always in his crib when Mom was torturing her muscles. Had he been kidnapped? Was Mom so busy sweating off calories that she hadn't even noticed?

I ran back into the living room. "Mom, Jasper's not in his crib!"

"I know, Mango," she said as she panted through push-ups. "Your father took him out."

"Oh," I said, thinking that was strange. This wasn't Dada's day off. What was he doing at home when he should be at Minelli's prepping for the dinner service? I shrugged and headed to my room to unload my backpack. If Dada had the day off for some reason, that would be cool, because I could tell him and Mom what had happened at the same time.

I dropped my backpack on my desk and threw myself onto the bed, crossing my hands behind my head. I stared up at the ceiling and started to sing to the crack that was shaped like Spider-Man, but I couldn't really hear myself with the exercise DVD booming from the living room. I leapt up from the bed, closed the door, put my fingers in my ears, and started singing "Halo" again, facing out the window.

I wanted to hear what I had sounded like in the auditorium. With my fingers in my ears, it was as though there was a soundproof chamber in my head, and I could hear myself really well. So well, in fact, that I didn't hear Dada knocking on my door, so I was startled—and a little embarrassed—when I turned around and saw him watching with Jasper in his arms. Dada was smiling, but I noticed something sad around his almond eyes.

"How long have you been standing there?"

"Long enough to see that you're in a particularly lovey-dovey mood today." He laughed. "Who's the lucky guy?"

"You," I said and stood on my toes to give him a peck on the cheek.

Jasper was hooting with his arms outstretched to me. I took him from Dada and planted kisses all over his chubby cheeks. "Come out into the living room. Your mom and I have something to tell you."

"I have something to tell you, too," I said as I followed him out of my room.

Mom was on the sofa toweling off, and Dada sat next to her. I plopped onto the floor in front of them, crisscross-applesauce, with Jasper on my lap.

Dada said, "You said you have something to tell us. Do you want to go first?"

"No," I said, "You go first. I'm saving the best for last."

Mom and Dada traded nervous glances and turned to me.

Mom cleared her throat and began, "Mango, we want you to know that none of this is your fault, honey. We want that to be clear."

A cloud must've passed over the sun, because all of a sudden the shafts of light through the blinds that made a pattern on the carpet disappeared. My mood darkened along with the room. You knew you're about to find out something really bad, maybe even bad enough to be life-changing, when your parents start a conversation like that. They would either say "Take a seat, honey," or "This is not as bad as it sounds, but . . ." Worst of all was the dreaded "This is not your fault."

So I braced myself. I held Jasper a little tighter than was comfortable for him and said, "What's not my fault?"

Dada put his hand on Mom's knee, signaling he'd take it from there. "I've been let go by the restaurant."

"Let go? You mean fired?"

Dada took a deep breath. "Yes. That's what I mean. But I don't want you to worry about—"

"Why did Mr. Minelli fire you? Was it because of me?"

Dada and Mom traded swift glances again, and then Mom said, "It's not your fault that her father can't separate business from his personal life. I suppose he's very protective of his child, and so are we."

"But Dada worked there way before I became friends with Brooklyn. Why—"

Dada slid off the couch and sat on the floor facing me. "Mango, honey, this was all my fault. I overheard the seafood delivery guy telling Mr. Minelli about some bully who stole his kid's bike. Then Minelli started in on how his daughter was the victim of a school bully who was jealous of her cell phone. Now see, I thought all this business was squashed after we'd replaced the phone and all, but . . . well, I just couldn't help myself. I asked him if he were referring to my daughter, because you are certainly not a bully. And, well, it all happened so fast. He admitted that he was talking about you, but not talking to me, so I should mind my own business, and I said, 'My daughter *is* my business' and . . . we exchanged a few more heated words. The next thing you know, he fired me."

My bottom lip began to tremble, and I curled it behind my teeth to stop it. Dada reached for my chin. "There's no need to worry. Everything will be fine. I can go back to catering until I get another job. In the meantime, I'll keep planning my own restaurant. We'll be fine."

"I'll go back to work sooner rather than later," Mom said. "Your father will be at home to look after Jasper for a while. Everything will work out; you'll see."

As much as I tried to stop it, I couldn't help the tears that dropped from my eyes and landed in Jasper's little Afro. "This is all my fault. You wouldn't have had to defend me if I hadn't been so stupid."

Dada took Jasper out of my arms and handed him to Mom. He put his arms around me and held me to his chest. "Mango, please don't blame yourself. I defended you because Mr. Minelli was wrong. I couldn't help myself. If anyone's to blame, it's me. But I don't have any regrets. I will defend you to the ends of the earth, no matter what, come what may. You are no bully. You're a good girl. My sweet *boonoonoonoos.*"

Jasper started getting cranky. Mom lifted his bottom to her nose, frowned, and took him away to change his diaper. Dada continued to rock me until my tears subsided. I lifted my head from his chest, and he looked at me with the most gentle smile on his face. "Okay, your turn. What's your news?"

I looked at him for a moment, not understanding what he was referring to. Then it came back to me: the audition. But all of the joy and excitement that had been bubbling inside me had gone flat. I said, "Nothing really. Nothing important. May I be excused now? I have a lot of homework to do."

Dada asked if I was sure, and I nodded yes. I got up from the floor and went to my room. Before entering, I looked back at Dada. He was still sitting on the floor with his shoulders hunched forward and his head down, and I knew the truth. Things were not as rosy as he and Mom were trying to make me believe. They were trying to protect me by making it seem as though we had nothing to worry about, but I could see that Dada was upset. I knew it was too soon for Mom to go back to work. The way her false leg had been hurting lately, it would be torture for her to keep it on all day.

I went straight to my bed and buried my face in the pillow. Things would be tough for all of us now. I decided that if I got cast in the play, I would turn it down. Then I would be able to come straight home after school every day and take care of Jasper while Dada looked for work or for investors in his restaurant or did catering jobs—if any of those came along. I wasn't even going to tell my parents about the audition. That way, if I were cast in *Yo, Romeo!* they wouldn't feel bad about my turning it down.

I felt proud that Dada believed in me enough to stand up to his boss, but I couldn't help thinking that if I'd never picked that phone up from the trash, none of this would ever have happened. Mom and Dada said they didn't blame me for all of our troubles, but I sure did.

CHAPTER 9

Spilled Beans

O n Dada's nights off from work, our dinner table was usually a laugh riot. Dada loved making us clutch our bellies with his seriously corny jokes and puns. Unfortunately, tonight the dominant sound around the table was the scraping of forks on plates as we all picked at our food. Even Jasper was not his usual bubbly self; he quietly mashed his peas as he picked them up one at a time and navigated them from the high chair tray to his mouth.

At about seven o'clock, the sound of the phone ringing cut through the silence. Dada went to answer it. I wondered if he was hoping, as I was, that Mr. Minelli would be on the phone, begging him to come back to work because the dinner rush was too much to handle without him. I listened closely to Dada's side of the conversation.

"Hello. Yes, this is the Fuller residence. Yes. This is her father. Uh-huh. Really? No, she didn't tell us anything about it." Dada turned to me with a quizzical expression. "Yes. Uh-huh. Yeah, I knew that, we all know, but . . . Uh-huh. Yes, my wife is here, we're all here. Okay. Hold on." Dada put his hand over the phone and said, "It's your teacher, Mr. Bob. He wants to be put on speaker so he can tell us all something at the same time. That all right with you, Mango?"

Unable to speak because I was taking a big gulp of iced tea when I heard Bob was on the phone, I nodded. Dada pressed the button for speaker and said, "Okay, you're on speaker."

Bob's voice burst into the room, loud and enthusiastic. "All right. Fantastic. Hi, Mango." I waved to the phone as if he could see me. "I was telling your father about your surprising audition this afternoon."

Mom's brow lifted as she looked at me. "Audition? What audition?" Dada shushed her.

"After a grueling casting session with my co-author, Larry—uh, Mr. Ramsey—we finally have the play cast. We fought tooth and nail over each role . . . except one. We immediately agreed that your voice is fantastic and you are our star. We want you to play Juliet."

Mom's hands flew to her mouth. Dada smiled, all of his beautiful white teeth with the gap in the middle sparkling at me from across the room. I gasped, and when I tried to speak the only thing that came out was a big, loud burp! Mom looked horrified. Dada turned away to keep from laughing out loud. I was so embarrassed. Had Bob heard that through the phone?

"Whoa," came through the speaker. "That was one big, healthy belch."

Yep, he heard.

"So what do you say, Mango? Are you up for being our star?"

I didn't know what to say. Mom and Dada stared at me, and even Jasper had stopped smushing his peas. They were all looking at me, waiting for an answer. I was stunned. I was confused. And all of a sudden, I was crying! Was I crying tears of joy at being cast in the leading role? Tears of fear at being offered the leading role in the school play? Tears of regret because I knew I had to turn down the role? Or were they tears of embarrassment? I guess I would have to say all of the above. My feelings were spinning, doing flips, and jerking all around like a crew of break-dancers.

Bob was still on the line. "Mango?"

Mom picked the phone up, took it off speaker, and spoke into the receiver. "Yes, she's okay. Just a little overwhelmed. Thank you so much for offering this opportunity to Mango. Let us talk it over, and Mango will let you know in the morning. Sure. Okay. Thanks for calling, Mr. Bob. Goodbye."

Dada sat down at the table as Mom clicked off the phone. Jasper smushed a handful of peas and threw them in my direction. I think they landed in my hair, but I was too bewildered to do anything about it. Dada leaned over to look in my eyes. "Why didn't you tell us you auditioned for the school play today?"

I cleared my throat and sipped my iced tea while my parents stared at me as if I were from Mars and waited for my answer. "I was going to tell you all about it, but after the news about your . . . your being let go from Minelli's, it just seemed so unimportant."

"Of course it's important, Mango. This is a great opportunity." Mom sat across from me and continued, "I always said you had a wonderful voice. I just never knew you wanted to sing or be in shows."

"I didn't. I don't."

"Really?" Dada said, with his head cocked to one side like a puppy's. "I always suspected you wanted to be onstage, otherwise why all those concerts in the bathroom every morning? Waking me up from a sound sleep, sounding like an angel—my own personal Beyoncé alarm clock."

"No, I don't. I can't sing in front of people."

Dada said, "But you auditioned. You must have wanted to at least try."

"I was tricked into auditioning. I think Brooklyn wrote my name on the list as a joke. As a way to embarrass me. But I didn't want to let her win, so I got up and sang."

Mom banged a fist on the table. "That's my girl! I'm so proud of you, honey."

"That's nice, Mom, but I'm not going to do the show. I'm going to turn it down."

"Oh, no you're not," she said.

"Why would you do that?" Dada asked, tilting his head to the other side.

I took a deep breath and looked at Dada. "Because with

83

you being out of work and Mom going back to work, I can't stay after school every day when I should be here helping with Jasper. You need me here, so you can have time to get your restaurant started and do your catering and whatever."

"Oh, honey, I would never ask you to give up something so wonderful. Trust me, you can be in the play. We'll be fine."

"But I don't want to be in the play!"

"Well, you shouldn't have auditioned," Mom said, standing up and putting her fists on her hips. "Once you stood on that stage and sang, you were committed. You know, I can't stand a quitter, Mango. This may be the one and only play you do in your entire life, but you gave your teachers a choice and they've chosen you. You are committed. I don't want to hear another word about quitting. You are going to play Juliet. Case closed." She picked up Jasper, his face and hair covered in green pea mush, and carried him away for his bath.

Dada and I watched Mom go. I turned to look at him. From his exasperated expression I believed I could spy a crack in their united front, so I poked my finger in it. "Do I really *have* to do the play, Dada? I never really wanted to be an actor or sing in front of people at all. I'm too afraid to do anything like that."

He stood and rubbed my shoulders. "It's up to you, Mango. You take your time tonight, think about it, and decide what you really want to do. I'll speak to your mother, and we'll abide by your decision." He started to leave the room but turned back. "You know, sweet one, fear can be a speed bump, a hill, or a mountain if you let it. But remember, any mountain can be climbed one step at a time."

After he left the kitchen, I just sat for a while trying to decide if the level of my fear was a speed bump, a hill, or a mountain. I started clearing the table, thinking about all that happened in just one day. I had gone from down in the dumps to higher than a cloud to sliding into a pit of depression only to be flung back up into the stars again. Talk about a roller coaster. This one had a three-hundred-fifty-degree loop de loop and a death drop!

As I washed the dishes, one thing made me smile: thinking of how foolish Brooklyn would feel when she found out her stupid prank had backfired and possibly made me the star of *Yo, Romeo!*

Lying in bed that night, I had a hard time falling asleep. Not because of the decision I had to make, but because I could hear my parents arguing in the next room. The sound was muffled, but I knew in my heart the argument was about me. My parents arguing always triggered my worst habit: biting my fingernails. As I've mentioned before, Mom was stubborn, and I knew she would not be satisfied until she got her way. She never "agreed to disagree" with Dada. I chewed the nails on my right hand to the nub while I lay in bed, trying to decide what would really be the best thing to do for my family.

CHAPTER 10
Yo, Romeo!

The next morning, as soon as I entered the lobby at school, I heard loud, high-pitched screaming. My bladder clenched. I turned around and around to see what kind of horrible thing had just happened and came face to face with Izzy and a crowd of kids stampeding toward me. They surrounded me, cheering. Izzy yanked me into a bear hug, shouting, "I told you so! I told you!"

The casting notice had just been posted, and the Dramanerds, who had been waiting all night to find out which parts they would play, had just learned that I'd been cast in the leading role. I was being passed around like a hot potato, getting hugs from all of my "new best friends." A few girls pulled me close, put their arms around my neck, smushed their faces up against mine, and took selfies of us.

I felt like a rock star might feel surrounded by fans and paparazzi. It was shocking and a little smothering, and just when my heart started pounding crazy fast and my palms got slick and my knees were about to turn to jelly, my teacher/director/bodyguard, Bob, broke through the mob and saved me. "All right. Back off, kids. Back off. You all should be on your way to your homerooms. I'll see you after school for our first company meeting and script distribution."

The cast and crew kids just stood there staring at me all starry-eyed. Bob clapped his hands together loudly. "Let's go! Let's go! Show me how well you can follow direction and beat it!" With that, they all scattered. All except Izzy. She gave me one last hug and whispered in my ear, "Told you so. You're going to be great."

When the mob was all gone, I noticed Brooklyn over by the cast list announcement, looking at me. When we made eye contact, she quickly turned away and stalked off down the hall. I must admit—that felt sweeeeeet!

Heading to my homeroom, Bob said, "First of all, I have to apologize for the feeding frenzy. Larry, I mean, Mr. Ramsey and I should have waited for your answer before we posted the casting notice. We were just so sure about you. . . . I guess we jumped the gun. Sorry."

I smiled. "It's okay."

He cleared his throat. "So? Did you think it over? Are you our Juliet? The star of *Yo, Romeo!*?" He stopped and turned to me with his hands up and then clasped them under his chin in a prayerful pose. "Before you say anything, please say yes! Please! You are the most exciting talent I've ever worked with in my life. Seriously, I'm talking semi-professional theater, college productions, and all my years teaching middle school,

I've never had the opportunity to work with a voice like yours. So, I'm begging. I swear, I'll get down on my knees if I must. Just, please, say yes."

Bob's overacting was funny and endearing, and I decided to end the suspense. I said, "Yes. Okay. I'll do it." Mom and Dada had been distant toward each other this morning. I knew Mom would hold a grudge against Dada for breaching their united front and not pressuring me to do the play. I thought saying yes would solve everything, so I did.

Bob leapt into the air, punching with his fist. "Yeah! All right!" His excitement was contagious, and his confidence in me gave me a glimmer of belief in myself. The rest of the school day was a blur. I could barely concentrate in any of my classes. Kids were congratulating me wherever I went.

Since I was now the queen of the Dramanerds, I had a place to sit in the cafeteria. All the chatter was about the play, which none of us knew much about except that it was based on *Romeo and Juliet* by William Shakespeare. Izzy said there was a good movie version starring Leonardo DiCaprio and Claire Danes. "I'll rent it and you can all come over on Saturday so we can watch it together!" High fives all around.

I didn't mean to, really, but I looked over at the Cellbelles' table. Brooklyn wasn't there. Hailey Joanne's crew was crowded over her shoulder, looking at something on her phone. She caught my eye, winked, and gave me a thumbs-up. I was like "huh?" but tried to eke out a smile and wink back at her—which was totally awkward. I mean, who winks at people except in breath mint commercials?

I couldn't help but wonder where Brooklyn was. I knew she was in school because I saw her this morning by the casting notice, but she wasn't in homeroom or language arts. It was odd that she wasn't seated next to her new bestie, Hailey Joanne, like she had been every day since getting her phone. Something told me there was trouble in paradise, but I didn't have much time to think about it, because Boss Chloe, the stage manager, ran up to the table and rasped with her blue hair and sandpaper voice, "Hey, did you see YouTube yet, dudes?"

Everyone who had phones pulled them out and started typing. I looked around to make sure the teachers on lunch duty weren't watching, but guess what? They were on their phones, too. Boss Chloe sat next to me, shoved her phone in front of my face and said, "Check this out!"

It was *me* on her screen, singing "Halo" in a video shot at the audition. I was, like, so amaze-face; eyes popping, mouth so wide open that flies could zip in and out. I don't think I took a breath while I watched. My heart was spinning like the mixer Dada uses to make cake batter, and I began to feel light-headed and woozy. My palms began to sweat, and my mouth filled up with that sour saliva that comes right before you greet your guts. I covered my mouth, bolted out of my seat, and dashed to the restroom.

I made it to the stall just in time to heave my tater tots,

chicken nuggets, and apple slices into the toilet bowl. Boss Chloe, Izzy, and Braces Chloe hurried in behind me. Boss Chloe took charge, ordering the other two girls to wet paper towels with cool water so she could press them to the back of my neck. When I was able to get to the sink to swoosh water and spit until my mouth felt clean, I asked, "How did I wind up on YouTube?"

Boss Chloe said, "My little birds told me Hailey Joanne uploaded it last night."

"Hailey Joanne? Seriously?"

"Chirp by the lockers is that H. J. and Brooklyn had a nasty argument about it, but Hailey Joanne went and did it anyway."

Izzy said, "That's so stray. Who would have thought Hailey Joanne would do anything nice for anyone except the zombies who follow her around like . . . zombies?"

"Please believe," Boss Chloe said as she patted another cool paper towel on my neck. "She did it to be monopular."

I peeled off the paper towel; it was starting to drip down my neck. "What?"

"*Monopular*. You know, having a monopoly on being popular."

"Did you just make that up?"

"Yep. I got a gift." Boss Chloe hiked up her cargo pants. "Seriously though, Mango, your audition is the talk of the school, and Hailey Joanne having it on video makes her the big mac without the spanks. So of course she uploaded it. She probably wants to be your BFBD."

I felt lame asking, but I did. "BFBD?"

All three of the girls clued me. "Best Friend By Default."

Boss Chloe said, "Everybody knows you're riding solo since you turned Brooklyn's phone into a submarine. So, H. J.'s gonna slide in and be relief pitcher—at least until the musical is over and the buzz around you dies down."

Izzy agreed. "Yeah, she'll brag that she was the one who made it all happen, when *I* was the one who brought you to the audition in the first place."

Braces Chloe, who was leaning against the door checking her phone, suddenly blurted out, "Wow, you've already got over six hundred views on YouTube, Mango. You're the biggest thing to happen to this school since Soy-Taco Tuesdays!"

While they were all congrats-hugging me, my stomach started feeling sour again. All the confidence Bob transfused into me had been flushed down the sewer with my vomit. Now that so many people knew about my being cast in the play, what if I failed? If I was a big flop, the whole YouTube-verse would know.

The bell rang. My head began to ache, so instead of going to my next class, I headed for the school nurse's office.

I needed a break and wanted to lie down in peace and quiet so I could get it together. Mrs. Totter, the nurse, was always sympathetic to girls with any kind of stomachache, so she let me lie down until I said I felt better, which was just after the final school bell rang.

On the way to the *Yo, Romeo!* company meeting, I started

beating up on myself. Was I insane? I should have never said yes. I had to hold onto the lockers while I walked down the hall. Stage fright was affecting my entire body, and I hadn't even made it to the stage yet.

If I couldn't walk into the auditorium on my own two feet, how was I ever going to dance and sing, or even speak, in front of an audience? An audience mostly made up of students ready to crank me through the meat grinder and launch tomatoes, pudding cups, and anything else they could sneak out of the cafeteria? I was just about to turn and rush out of the building when Izzy appeared and looped her arm through mine.

"I know what you're thinking, and you're not taking off." I shook my head, but she didn't buy it. "Don't try to smoke-screen me, rookie. I can tell by the death stare in your eyes, your dry lips, and the way you're trembling like you just got a brain freeze from a Slurpee. You're terrified. Am I right, or am I right?"

"You're right."

"Of course I am. But listen—you don't have anything to worry about. This is just a company meeting. Bob will probably start off by talking about the show, and then Mr. Ramsey will play a few songs with Bob singing along—that's always *high*-larious. Finally, they'll introduce the cast, calling us up onstage one by one, handing out the scripts, and telling us to read the entire thing over the weekend—not just the scenes we're in. Then everyone will rush off home to count their lines and highlight their scripts. *Finito*. So easy-peasy, quit being cheesy." With that, Izzy led me into the auditorium, and my life in the theater began.

Bob and Mr. Ramsey walked onto the stage to wild applause. They bowed and joked and did the *yada, yada, yada* about how happy they were that we were finally ready to start rehearsals on the greatest musical they'd ever collaborated on, which was based on the tragedy written by Shakespeare, the greatest playwright who ever lived, and how *Yo, Romeo!* was going to be the most amazing show the school had ever seen!

Bob began telling us about *Romeo and Juliet*, the Shakespeare play. The story was about a boy, Romeo, and a girl, Juliet, who fell in love even though their families were sworn enemies. They sneaked off and got married in secret. Then there was a lot of fighting, and Romeo accidentally killed one of Juliet's cousins and was kicked out of town. A friar, which is like a priest, gave Juliet a potion that made her seem dead so she could stop her wedding to some other dude her parents wanted her to marry. When Romeo found her, he thought she really was dead, so he killed himself. When Juliet woke up, she was so depressed that she killed herself with Romeo's knife.

The story is seriously cray-cray.

Just before we were about to zone out listening to Bob talk about the Shakespeare play, he switched gears and began explaining. "Our musical is loosely—*very* loosely—

based on Shakespeare's play. *Yo, Romeo!* takes place in the 1990s." That got a huge response from the cast, because we all were obsessed with how funny things were back when our parents were young. I'd spent hours laughing with Mom and Dada, looking through photo albums that had pictures of Dada with bleached hair, thick, ropey gold chains around his neck, and a leather eight-ball jacket. Some were of Mom at school wearing baggy overalls and platform sneakers, and there was one of her going to a party dressed like a Spice Girl! OMGZ, *high*-larious!

Our attention revived, Bob continued, "Romeo is a rocker, like Bruce Springsteen, and Juliet is a pop star—a cross between Mariah Carey and Beyoncé." I gasped. I would be playing a part based partially on my favorite singer! I sat up in my seat, excitement filling me up the way the soda fountain fills a cup at Mickey D's.

"Romeo and Juliet are both signed with rival record companies run by their families. They fall in love and secretly record some songs together, even though their families forbid it. The head of Romeo's record company hears about this and thinks recording with a pop star will turn Romeo's hard-rock fan base against him and hurt his record sales, so he starts a rumor online that Juliet is dead. Romeo believes the rumor— but this is a middle-school production, and we can't have our stars committing suicide. So just before Romeo swallows some poison, he gets a text from Juliet. The text tells him to meet her at the airport, where she's hired a private plane that flies them off to live happily ever after . . . but the plane goes down in the Bermuda Triangle, and they are never seen again. Their families get together to lament the loss of their children and agree to release the secret recordings Romeo and Juliet made, which become huge hits that make our star-crossed lovers live on forever."

While listening to the story, I realized that I'd never even thought about who was going to play Romeo, the boy I'd have to pretend to be in love with and maybe even kiss! OMGZ, I was definitely *not* into kissing for the very first time while a bunch of people watched.

Bob began calling the cast to the stage. First he announced the members of the chorus, who went up onstage one by one to applause. Then he announced the supporting cast. Izzy was cast as Juliet's agent, who secretly helps her get to the recording studio with Romeo—sort of like the nurse in the Shakespeare original.

Bob called me up to the stage. The cast applauded wildly. I must admit, it felt kind of good that they were excited about welcoming me to their world. As long as they were on my side, I got the feeling being in a play wouldn't be so bad.

The only ones left in the seats were students we called the Downbeats. They usually played in the orchestra and marching band. Finally, Bob called for TJ Gatt to come to the stage. TJ was tall and lanky with a kind of intense face. I didn't know him personally at all, but I'd heard about him. He was a grade ahead of me, and he was the lead singer and guitar player of a rock band called the Halfrican Americans. All the band members—two guys, one who played keyboard and one who played bass, and a girl drummer named Natsuko—were biracial. TJ was black and Italian, and Natsuko was Japanese and Puerto Rican. I wasn't sure about the other two guys, but I guess they were a pretty good group, because they played at a lot of parties and festivals and no one heckled or threw things at them.

TJ was a quiet guy, sort of a loner who only hung out with his band and never said much of anything to anyone else. The fact that he had tried out for the play was a huge surprise, which Bob quickly cleared up. "We had to chase this guy down to get him to audition in private, but we wanted someone we knew could rock out and act, and in TJ, I know we've found our man."

All the kids, including me, applauded as TJ loped up to the stage wearing dark glasses that hid his eyes, a T-shirt, torn jeans, and a leather jacket that was pretty beat up but in a cool way. He had frizzy black hair that he wore in a Mohawk. He stood next to me, and I had to look way up to see his face. He didn't turn to me or smile or anything, so I turned away from him and wondered what I had gotten myself into. Would I really have to pretend to be in love with this scary guy? Would I have to kiss him?

Mr. Ramsey and Bob handed us our scripts. I knew that

as soon as I got home, I would scan through the pages to make sure I didn't have any kissing scenes with TJ. If I did, I'd have to google "dying of embarrassment" to see if it were a real possibility.

I was walking with Izzy as everyone headed out of the auditorium when Mr. Ramsey called for TJ and me to stay behind. Izzy closed her eyes and shimmied as if she had swallowed the best ice cream ever. "You are so crazy lucky. You get to fall in love with TJ. He's so cute—not, like, ordinary cute but kind of scary-weird-cute. You know what I mean? Anyway, I'll call you about the movie at my house tomorrow. See ya."

She hurried out of the auditorium, leaving me alone with TJ while Mr. Ramsey went to get something from his office. TJ was sitting on the edge of the stage, so I went down the aisle and sat across from him in the front row. As far as I could tell, he wasn't looking at me from behind his dark glasses, so I didn't look at him even though I wanted to see what he really looked like. It's bizzarro, I know, but until I got into a situation with people—like in the same class or assigned to a study group—I didn't really notice much about them. It's like when you go to the movies: you watch the stars, *not* the people sitting in the background drinking coffee or walking by on the street. So I had never really taken a good look at TJ before. He'd been a background person in my life until today.

Mr. Ramsey returned with two large envelopes and

handed one to each of us. "You've both got great, challenging solos and duets, so we're going to be seeing a lot of each other over the next seven weeks." He turned to me and said, "With a voice like yours . . . do you read?"

I smirked. "Of course I read."

"Great. That will make all our lives a lot easier. Take some time this weekend and go over the music. We'll have our first private rehearsal Monday after school." He gave a sort of stiff salute and took off, leaving TJ and me alone in the auditorium together.

I was about to leave when TJ jumped down from the stage and headed toward me. He stopped right in front of me and said, "Uh, hi."

I said, "Hi."

He said, "Nice to meet you."

"Nice to meet you, too."

We stood surrounded by an awkward silence for what seemed like forever before he said, "Did you, uh . . . Didja know the smallest monkey in the world is about as tall as a toothbrush?"

I stared at him for a moment, shook my head, and said, "Uh . . . what?"

He looked at his boots, shrugged, and said, "Right. Okay then. See ya." And he took off up the aisle and out of the auditorium, leaving me completely confused-dot-com. What just happened? What did toothbrush-size monkeys have to do with anything? Was he trying to say I was short? Or looked like a freaky monkey? I decided to sit right back down where I was, skim the script, and make sure I had no kissing scenes with Mister Scary-Weird-Cute!

CHAPTER 11

Yo, Juliet!

It turns out I *did* have a kissing scene with TJ—or should I say Romeo? Only one kiss, but still, OMGZ! There was a scene where Romeo and Juliet fall in love singing a duet, and according to the script, they kiss as the lights fade to black.

How could Bob do this to me? Or any girl? Who would want to kiss a complete stranger in front of the whole entire school? We were only scheduled to do the show for one weekend—Friday and Saturday nights and Sunday afternoon. One kiss per show. . . . That meant three kisses! And that wasn't counting rehearsals.

Thinking about it on the way home while gnawing on my bottom lip like it was hamburger (of course, I stopped when I realized no one would want to kiss hamburger lips), I recognized that after seven weeks of rehearsal, TJ and I wouldn't be strangers anymore. We'd probably be friends. Maybe even good friends. And that might make it easier to kiss him, or worse. . . . What could be more embarrassing than kissing a boy who was your friend? That could make the friendship really awkward.

When I got home, Dada had taken Jasper out to the park, and Mom was huffing her way through *Muscle Torture*, so I went straight to my room and opened the envelope Mr. Ramsey had given me. There were five songs on sheet music. I got a sinking feeling when I remembered him asking, "Do you read?" He must have meant do I read *music*! Of course I don't. This was going to make rehearsal even harder. I couldn't learn any songs from dots sprinkled across pages full of lines.

On Saturday afternoon, the whole company gathered in Izzy's basement to watch Leonardo DiCaprio and Claire Danes in *Romeo + Juliet*. Before the movie started, Izzy called me up to her bedroom, where Boss Chloe and Braces Chloe were waiting. Izzy said in a very serious tone, "Sit down, Mango. We've got something heavy to tell you."

I sat on the edge of the bed. "What? Did something happen?"

The girls turned to Boss Chloe, who shook her blue head mournfully, as if she were watching a casket being lowered into a grave. "I hate to tell you this, but the chirp on the street is that Brooklyn has left the building."

"What building? She was here, in Izzy's house?"

"No. She left Trueheart Middle School and transferred to Islington."

I couldn't believe it. Brooklyn transferred to the private school that was GOT's biggest rival? "How do you know?"

Boss Chloe shrugged. "What can I say? My little birds. . ."

Izzy sat down next to me on the bed and took my hands into hers. "It's factual. I saw Brooklyn and her mother drive by this morning with an Islington Superiors sticker on the back of their SUV." She patted my hands. "We thought you should know, seeing as how you two were besties and all."

Boss Chloe hiked up her blue cargo shorts and said, "Actually, her defecting is tragically delicious. You won't have to worry about her spreading bad karma or playing dirty tricks on you anymore."

I nodded, still trying to comprehend Brooklyn getting her parents to send her to private school because a trick she played on me backfired. I thought she was tougher than that, but I guess I really didn't know her as well as I thought. From then on, I was going to be über careful about who I got close to and who I let get close to me.

Braces Chloe held out her phone to me. "On a brighter note, you've got over fifteen hundred hits on YouTube."

Fifteen hundred? That means people have watched my audition more than one thousand times. That's more people than I've ever spoken to in my entire life! I was almost semi-famous. Suddenly goose pimples were spreading all over my arms.

"This is epic," Boss Chloe said. "What you need to do now is grow your fan base on Instagram, Twitter, Snapchat,

Facebook, and all the rest. I heard that colleges take how many followers you have into consideration for acceptance and scholarships."

I said, "But I don't have any of those!"

"Not even Facebook?"

Izzy said, "It's not her fault. She doesn't have a phone, and her parents are kind of social media–phobes."

I nodded; it was true, although I didn't want the world to know.

Boss Chloe winced. "Ouch! Dude, you're in Social Siberia. That stinks." She shook her head, pacing while looking down at the floor. "How am I s'posed to text you about rehearsals and last-minute schedule changes?"

Izzy stepped forward. "Send them to me, boss. I'll make sure she's up to date."

"Thanks, Izzy." I was grateful but embarrassed for feeling like the other girls were pitying me. Even as a Dramanerd star, I was an oddball because I didn't have a phone.

Izzy patted me on the back. "Let's go to the basement and start the movie. We've got popcorn, juice, and hot herbal tea— in case your voice is getting tired from learning your songs."

As we headed down to the basement, I asked for a tea so everyone would think I was rehearsing my songs, even though I really had no idea how to start and was too ashamed to ask for help.

Izzy's basement had the biggest flat-screen TV I had ever seen. TJ and a bunch of the Downbeats were on couches, so

I slumped onto a beanbag way on the other side of the room. The movie was surprisingly good, but it was so embarrassing every time Romeo and Juliet kissed. Everyone would whoop it up, looking back and forth between me and TJ on opposite sides of the basement. I don't know about him, but I kept staring straight ahead at the screen, pretending to be totally absorbed by the movie. In reality, my head was throbbing thinking about the kissing and how dumb I felt about not being able to read music.

After the movie was over, most of the cast stayed to hang out with Izzy. I wanted to stick around, too. Everyone was so nice, and I was having more fun than I'd had since my friend-life was all about Brooklyn, but I had to get home by five o'clock. Mom and Dada were going to stop by a few restaurants and eat appetizers while checking to see if there were any openings in the kitchens, which was way cooler than Dada just showing up and handing them his résumé.

As I was leaving the basement, TJ was heading back downstairs. We nodded as we passed each other, and for a brief second I thought I had made a clean getaway, but he called to me from the bottom of the stairs. "How'd you like the songs?"

"The songs?"

"Yeah. I was playing around with them on my keyboard. They're pretty tight, I mean, for pop/rock songs, right?"

Since I couldn't read music and had no idea what the songs were like, I lied. "Oh, yeah. Awesome!" What else could

I do? I was a musically illiterate twit staring down at a scary-weird-cute guy, whom I just realized had kiwi-green eyes.

Ugh, I love kiwi.

"Which is your favorite?"

"Uhhhh . . . ummmm . . ." I ransacked my brain trying to remember a song title and blurted out the first one that came to my head. "'Looking Up at Love'! That song really fits my voice well. I can't wait to sing it with the band and everything. . . ."

"Really?"

"Yeah. I'm working on the words and melody and, you know . . . the beat and stuff already."

He stared up at me for what felt like a half a minute. The kids back in the basement were laughing at something, and I kind of got the idea it was me they were laughing at even though the thought was ridiculous—there was no way they could hear me lying to TJ on the staircase. Then I swallowed and realized the hot tea tasted like licorice, which I loved, especially the little piece of licorice in Good & Plenty candy, so I'd have to ask Mom to buy some. . . . Just before my brain whirled off to some other random thought, TJ said, "You know, there was this chicken once, I think his name was Mike, and he lived for eighteen months without a head."

I said, "Uhhhhhh. Okay."

TJ shrugged, turned, and headed into the basement without another word. So I continued up the stairs, out of the house, and walked down the block, wondering if this scary-weird-cute-kiwi-green-eyed guy was trying to say I was a chicken with her head cut off!

My actual salvation came the next morning while I was sitting at my desk highlighting my script. All the kids in the cast were highlighting their scripts when we were at Izzy's, so I got out my lavender highlighter and went through my script highlighting all the lines. I wasn't sure why they did this. Maybe because it made the script look more colorful and that could help with your acting?

I was almost at the end of my lavender script when Mom came into my room saying, "Something strange just happened."

"What?"

"Well . . ." She looked at me quizzically and said, "There was a knock at the door. I went to open it and no one was there. But this envelope with your name on it was on the welcome mat."

I agreed; that *was* strange. Then my turbo-psycho imagination kicked in. Could it be a letter bomb? Or maybe it was filled with anthrax, that powder poison that can kill you just by touching your skin. I got up from my chair and backed away from Mom. "Quick, throw it out the window and call 9-1-1. It could be dangerous. Lethal!"

"Lethal? Don't be silly, Mango. Who would want to kill you?"

Hmm . . . That was something to think about. For starters, I wouldn't have been surprised if Brooklyn had put a hit out on me since it turned out the joke was on *her* when I won the lead in the musical and because my success had caused a riftin her wicked *fiendship* with Hailey Joanne. Yep. Brooklyn could possibly be out to get me. I said, "Hold the envelope up so I can see the handwriting."

Mom rolled her eyes as she held up the envelope. Nope. It wasn't Brooklyn. Not her handwriting. I sighed and started toward Mom but stopped, thinking Brooklyn could have hired an assassin to write my name just to throw me off.

"Mango . . ." Mom's lips twisted impatiently. "Are you going to open this thing or not?"

"Okay. Okay . . ." I took the envelope. It was very light and flat. Nobody could make a bomb that small. I ran my hands over it, trying to identify the contents. There *was* something in there about the size of a tube of lipstick but flat. Weird. I sniffed the envelope very tentatively. Nothing smelled like poison—whatever poison smelled like. As I held the envelope up to the light, Mom snatched it out of my hand.

"Enough!" She ripped the envelope open, and a zip drive fell onto the floor. I ducked behind my bed. "Mango, stop being so silly. Slide it into the laptop and see what's on it."

I stood and picked it up with the tip of two fingers, holding it as far away from my body as possible. Just before inserting it into the laptop, I asked, "What if it has a virus?"

Mom threw her hands into the air, sighed, and headed out of the room. "I give up. Do what you want with it. I'm through."

I sat staring at the zip drive in my hand for the longest time before finally inserting it into the computer. I rolled away from the desk, expecting a horrific skull and crossbones to appear on the screen, glaring as the virus ate all of my Beyoncé albums and destroyed my hard drive.

But none of that happened. Instead, a file appeared. It was titled "Yo, Juliet/Scratch Tracks."

I clicked it open. In it were all of the songs Mr. Ramsey had sent home with me but on MP3 files. I opened the first one: "Duet Forever." A piano played, and I heard TJ's voice singing. He sounded great, but I kind of giggled when he sang my part, because when he sang in a high falsetto, his voice would crack. I hoped that wasn't the way I sounded to him. Then I realized he'd never heard me sing—well unless he'd seen the video on YouTube, which now had over twenty-eight hundred hits and a ton of comments, really positive ones. I wondered who these people were and wished I could thank every one of them.

I spent the rest of the afternoon listening to all the songs. TJ must have figured out that I couldn't read music, because the song I said was my favorite—the one I "couldn't wait to sing"—was Romeo's solo! Great. Now he probably saw me as a music illiterate and a bad liar. So why did he go out of his way to help me?

After dinner, I worked on learning the songs. At least, I tried, but my mind kept wandering off to TJ, wondering why he recorded the songs for me and thinking about how it was such a sweet thing to do. It was getting easier and easier to imagine him as Romeo.

At our first rehearsal, the cast sat crisscross-applesauce on the stage floor in a large circle and read the script out loud. I wish Izzy had warned me about this, because I was totally unprepared to say things like, "Baby, you're the most beautiful boy in the world to me," or "I've never felt love like this before," or worst of all, "Yo, Romeo, what are you waiting for? Kiss me!" I was probably as purple as a plum.

My biggest problem during the read-through was that I could barely be heard. Bob kept asking me to "project" and "share my voice." I tried, but since he had to keep repeating himself, I don't think I was making much progress. Izzy had no problem projecting. People in Timbuktu could probably hear her lines. Now, my singing voice was very loud, so I just had to figure out a way to speak from the same place I sang from—another thing I had to work on in addition to learning lines, songs, and how to act. Thank goodness there wasn't much spoken dialogue in the play (most of it was in song), so the read-through wound up being pretty short.

Bob started "blocking" the first act. Izzy explained that blocking was mapping out where everyone would stand and move during a scene. She showed me a cool shortcut way to mark it in my script with a pencil so I could keep up with Bob and all the changes he kept making.

However, when Izzy saw my script and how lavender it all

was, she whispered, "Girl, you're only supposed to highlight *your* lines, not everyone's lines and all the stage directions."

I would have felt completely humiliated if she hadn't whispered, keeping it private between us. Still, I held my script close to my chest, hoping no one else saw how green I was.

Izzy was kind and thoughtful and did her best to encourage me throughout the rehearsal. I wondered how we had lost touch after kindergarten. She was the kind of friend a girl like me needed. I promised myself I would be as good a friend to Izzy as she was to me. Maybe we'd become besties one day, but I was determined to take it slow.

About an hour into blocking, Boss Chloe sent TJ and me to the music room to work with Mr. Ramsey on our first duet. On the way down the staircase, I got up the courage to thank him for the scratch tracks. He nodded and smiled. It became clear to me that this scary-weird-cute-kiwi-green-eyed guy was probably just as shy as I was. That helped me relax a little.

At the door to the music room, TJ asked, "Did you work on the songs?"

I smiled. "Yes. Constantly."

"Cool. So, there's no need to tell Ramsey you don't read music. He's a real snob when it comes to musicianship. If you don't know the melody, fake it."

"I will. Thanks."

The hardest part of our first music rehearsal was trying to stop my hands from shaking while holding the sheet music. But I was grateful to have the music to glance at as an excuse not to look at TJ. Mr. Ramsey was encouraging us to sing to each other—after all, it was a duet, and we were supposed to act like we were falling in love. Still, even though I had memorized most of the words to this song over the weekend, I kept my eyes on the page. I wasn't ready to look at TJ, or any boy, with "lovey-dovey eyes."

After rehearsal, I met up with Izzy. We were now "walk home" buddies. We had a lot to talk about; mostly about the show and who was bonding with whom in the cast. We weren't yet at the point where we talked for hours on the phone. I was still taking my time, letting our friendship develop. But I could see us burning up the phone lines in the near future.

Izzy came with me to my locker, where I was stunned and a little bit scared to see Hailey Joanne. Her back was to me, and she was on her phone, but she was definitely leaning on my locker. I stopped in my tracks and actually gulped. Izzy nudged me forward. "Don't let her see you sweat. Remember, you're the star now."

I took a deep breath, put my shoulders back, and carried on. She must have heard us approaching, because she turned, clicked off her phone, tossed her thick, raven, Korean, human-hair weave and gave me a huge smile. "Mango! I've been looking all over for you. How was rehearsal?"

I tried to speak, but my tongue was acting as if I'd just swallowed a jar of super-chunky peanut butter. Izzy came to my rescue. "Rehearsal was great. Mango is going to be the biggest star this school has ever seen."

"School? Isabel, she's way bigger than the school already, thanks to the video I uploaded on YouTube. You do know it was me who put it out there, don't you?"

I nodded like a dunce.

"You have over four thousand hits as of the last time I checked, which was about twenty minutes ago." She tossed back her thick locks. They must've cost her a fortune. "I hope you didn't mind my posting it, Mango. You were just so great, I couldn't help myself. I guess I should have asked you first, but you know me—super impulsive."

Actually, I didn't know her. And I didn't understand why she was talking to me and assuming that I knew anything about her. Unsure of what to say, I flexed my cheek muscles into something resembling a smile and nodded.

"So, anyway, you know my thirteenth birthday gala is next month, and I wanted to invite you." She reached into her trendy bag that probably cost quadruple my entire school clothing allowance for the year and pulled out a mint-green envelope. "Please excuse the old-fashioned invite, but Mother is so traditional. I mean, you'd think I was getting married for all the trouble and expense she went through."

Izzy took the envelope and slipped it under my arm. "Oh, come on, H. J., don't begrudge Mommy a chance to show off."

Hailey Joanne shot a ballistic glance at Izzy and said, "It's *Hailey Joanne*. You may think calling people by their initials is cool, but, believe me, it's not. I don't like it. Call me by my name or don't call me at all." As her neck swerved toward me, she smiled. "I hope you can make it, Mango. It's going to be downtown at the Rivoli Hotel, in the grand ballroom. Everybody who's anybody is going to be there. I'm going to have live entertainment and catered food, and some celebrity friends of my father have promised to drop by."

Hailey Joanne's father owned a limousine company and a car dealership, so it was probable that he knew celebrities. Hailey Joanne was dropped off and picked up from school daily by a chauffeur in a luxury SUV with tinted windows.

"Say you'll come, Mango. You can bring a friend if you want."

"Yes! She'll come." Izzy blurted wrapping her arm around my shoulder.

Hailey Joanne leaned back on her hip and looked Izzy over. "What, she can't speak for herself?"

"Of course, she can speak," Izzy replied, "but she's saving her voice. After a long rehearsal, those golden pipes need a rest. Know what I'm sayin'?"

"Of course. Well . . ." Hailey Joanne flashed a dazzling smile at Izzy that was all teeth with absolutely no connection to her eyes. "Instead of presents, we're asking everyone to make a donation to a charity in my name. It doesn't matter which charity. Whatever you usually donate to is fine." Her bedazzled phone trilled. She put it to her ear, purred a greeting while fluttering her fingers in our direction, and headed off down the hall.

With the phantom peanut butter finally dissolving in my

mouth, I turned on Izzy. "How could you accept her invitation for me?"

"Hey, you weren't saying anything, and when she said you could bring a guest . . . well, I sure want to go. Don't you?"

"No. Not really. I don't. She's not my friend. She's just being a BFBD because of the YouTube thing."

"So what?" Izzy said, her head swiveling from side to side with mucho savvy-tude. "The least we could do is take advantage. You know what my tía Maria Magdelena said before her tragic car crash? 'When someone hands you phony baloney, fry it up and chow down!'"

I couldn't help but smile as I turned away and opened my locker. Izzy went on, "Do you know who was at her last birthday party? Gabriel Faust, that's who! Are you going to miss a chance to rub elbows with a star?"

I bit my lip. Gabriel Faust . . . Who wouldn't want to meet a mega-star like him? I had a life-size poster of him on the inside of my closet door, so whenever I opened it, it was like he was there waiting to greet me. I had followed him since I was six—from boy band to TV star to solo singing sensation. I was beginning to lean toward yes, but I wavered. "I don't have a charity. I mean, really, my father just lost his job."

"Oh, don't worry about it. You can donate ten dollars to some cause in her name and they'll send her a card saying you donated for so-and-so, but they won't mention how much. She'll never know. Relax. I got you, girl."

I took my backpack from my locker and dropped the

invitation into the outer pocket. As we walked out of the school my fingernails began to tingle. I wanted to chew on them as I tried to think of a way out of this whole birthday-party thing. Not that I didn't like birthday parties, but I was used to regular parties for regular people. That's me; I'm just a regular people. I'd feel awkward hanging out at the Rivoli Hotel with that glitzy crowd, the ones you see pictures of in the newspaper with captions about the dazzling affair they were attending. All the ladies would be in designer gowns and dresses with a mask of makeup. Reporters would ask, "Who are you wearing?" How would I answer that question truthfully? "I'm wearing the fifth-grade graduation dress my mother got on discount."

Izzy gabbed on about how great the party would be all the way to her house while I secretly decided that I was not going. I'd give her my invitation if she wanted it, but Mango Delight Fuller was not about to make a fool of herself in front of all of those society people. Besides, what if Hailey Joanne and Brooklyn had pretended they were fighting just to set me up? What if they were planning on dropping a bucket of blood on my head, like in that horror movie *Carrie*? No. There was no way I was going to subject myself to that kind of humiliation. That was one trap this mouse was definitely going to avoid.

CHAPTER 12

Mission Improbable

The invite must've fallen on the floor when I was unloading my backpack. I mean, how else could Jasper have gotten hold of it? When Mom brought it to the table where Dada and I were just finishing our dinner, one corner of the mint-green envelope was gummed and covered with slobber.

"Mango, you have to be more careful about things you leave on the floor." She held out the envelope. "What's this?"

"Uh . . . I don't know."

"You don't know? How can you not know when someone went to the trouble of writing your name with beautiful calligraphy? Looks like a professional job . . . with gold leaf and everything."

"It's just a birthday party invitation," I mumbled.

Mom said, "Who's having a birthday? The Queen of Sheba?"

Dada's left eyebrow arched. "I thought everyone sent electronic invitations nowadays."

Mom shook her head and smirked. "Everybody except

people with money to burn and attitude for kindling." She and Dada laughed.

I was beginning to get irritated and pushed my plate away. "It doesn't matter. I'm not going."

Dada looked up from wiping crusty Italian bread into his homemade marinara sauce. "Why not?"

"I'm over birthday parties."

He raised both eyebrows as he bit into the bread. "Since when?"

"Since now, Dada. Let it go, please."

Mom eyed me suspiciously before sliding her finger under the flap of the envelope. I reached for it. "What are you doing?"

"I just want to see. Why should it matter if you're not going?" she said and pulled out the fanciest invitation I'd ever seen.

The card had a thin paper overlay that looked like lace, and on the cover under that was a photo of Hailey Joanne wearing a tiara and her six-hundred-tooth, fifty-watt smile. "My goodness," Mom said. "This is a fancy affair. In the ballroom at the Rivoli. What a waste of money on a birthday party. Each of these invitations must've cost ten dollars."

"Who is the party for?" Dada asked as he poured a little more iced tea into his glass.

I sighed. "Hailey Joanne."

"Pinkey?"

"Yes."

"Wow," Dada said and took a long swallow of iced tea. "Minelli's catered the Pinkeys's anniversary party last year. It was a huge affair; the restaurant made thousands just from that one gig. I created the menu, did the prep, supervised the cooking, hired extra servers, and I wound up getting a really nice tip. Mr. Pinkey said I was impressive." He finished the last of his iced tea and got up from the table. "I wonder if they've hired a caterer for the birthday party yet. Sure would be nice to swoop in and pick up a gig like that." He shoved his hands into his pockets and left the kitchen.

I nearly jumped out of my sneakers when Mom cried out, "Oh my goodness! Boy! What in the world . . . ?"

I turned to Jasper, who had turned his bowl of pasta upside down—on his head. Marinara sauce dripped down his face, and pasta hung on his head like long hair. Jasper laughed and clapped his hands. I couldn't help it; the little round brown clown had me laughing, too. Even Mom chuckled as she took the bowl off his head, lifted him out of his high chair, and held him at arm's length as she hurried down the hall to the bathroom.

I began clearing the table and smiled to myself as I thought about my crazy family and how much fun we had, especially when we were all together. I knew it wasn't right, since Dada was out of work and all, but I had to admit I was enjoying having him home more. I mean, he wasn't as lighthearted as he usually was. He had a lot on his mind. I wished he could get that job catering Hailey Joanne's party. . . . I stopped clearing the table.

An idea burst into my brain like a million gazillion fireworks. I could help him get the job. I could ask Hailey Joanne, you know, like just casually bring it up in conversation. Say something like, "Do you already have a caterer for your party? By the way, my father is an excellent caterer."

"Oh yeah, great, Mango, that's *real* casual," I said to myself out loud.

"What's real casual?"

I turned, startled to see Dada standing behind me. I swear he moved quieter than a ghost. It took a few seconds of "uh . . . um . . . uhhhhh . . ." before I blurted out, "My lines—I was working on my lines for the play. A line that's supposed to be said really casual, like . . . 'Hey, um, buddy, how are you doing today?' But I don't think I've figured out a way to say it casual enough yet. Ha-ha."

Dada just studied me for a few seconds and then said, "Just throw it away. You know, don't think about it. Like this: *Hiyah, rude-bwoy, how it gwan today, bruddah?*"

I giggled. "Yeah, well, it's not *Romeo and Juliet* in Jamaica, Dada." I got back to clearing the table. He grabbed the bowl out of my hand.

"Let me do that, honey. You go finish your homework and study your lines."

I stood on my tiptoes and gave him a peck on the cheek. Dada grabbed his cheek and swooned. "Kissed by a star! I'll never wash this cheek again!"

I left the kitchen laughing. My dada, Sidney Ricardo

Fuller, was the sweetest man in the whole wide world, and I was going to do whatever I could to get him hired to cater for Hailey Joanne's birthday party.

As soon as that thought crystallized in my mind, a mango pit plopped into my belly. How? How would I convince Hailey Joanne Pinkey to hire Dada to cater her grand affair? Since the YouTube thing, she'd been acting as if we were friends, so maybe I could act like we really *were* friends and . . .

No, there was no way I could do it. I wasn't that good of an actor. The thought of actually having a "casual" conversation with the queen diva herself lured my index finger to my teeth and the nail-gnawing began.

But then again . . . how could I *not* do it? Or at least take a stab at it. This would be a big chance for Dada to prove himself and change his life. It could even lead to his dream of having his own restaurant. Someway, somehow, I would have to find the courage to face Hailey Joanne, pretend to be her friend, and agree to go to her party. Maybe then she would be fake-kind enough to give Dada a chance.

I didn't get a shot at speaking to Hailey Joanne one-on-one either Tuesday or Wednesday. I knew the clock was ticking, and the event was getting closer with each passing day. Finally on Thursday, after a brutal dance rehearsal (natural rhythm must have skipped a generation with me), I bumped into Hailey Joanne in the girls' locker room. She was changing after GOT, and I was so sweaty that I had to shower and change my clothes, too.

She asked if I was excited about the party. I did my best to pretend to be excited when I said, "Yes, it's practically the only thing I've been thinking about besides the play and school, I guess."

"I'm so glad you're coming. Do you know what you're wearing?"

"Uh, no. My thoughts haven't gotten that far yet."

Hailey Joanne actually put her finger on her chin, tilted her head, struck a thinking pose, and said, "Why don't you come over to my house this afternoon? My stylist pulled some dresses from all the best stores. It'll be fun—our very own private fitting. We can try everything on and pretend we're supermodels. It'll be über crisp."

"Uh . . ."

"I won't take no for an answer. You can use my phone to call your parents. My car is waiting out front at the curb. Hurry now—fashion waits for no girl!" Fingers fluttering, she darted out of the locker room.

I sank down onto the bench. What had I gotten myself into? I knew I could never afford a designer dress. There was no point of going to her house . . . except that it might give me the chance to bring up the caterer thing and take a chance at helping Dada. I had to suck it up, quit being a wimp, and put myself out there for the family.

The chauffeur, Mr. Versey—a very distinguished older gentleman with jet-black hair and a snow-white mustache— drove us to a part of town I'd only ridden through on the way to the airport. Actually, I'd only ridden *by* this neighborhood on the freeway, never on the actual streets, which were tree lined. There were no sidewalks. All the houses were about a block apart, behind gates, and surrounded by walls. They were the kind of houses you'd see on real-estate reality shows that took place in Beverly Hills. The trip was about an hour long, which made me wonder why Hailey Joanne would drive so far to go to Trueheart, a public school, when she could have her pick of ultra-private schools closer to her own home. Maybe it would have been harder to be the queen diva at a school with other girls just as rich or richer than she was.

There was a large circular driveway in front of the red brick house. No—it was more than a house. Izzy and Brooklyn lived in houses. *This* was a mansion. I didn't know much about cars, but there was a car in the driveway that had doors that opened up like wings along with a couple of limousines and two motorcycles that looked like something Batman would ride.

A butler opened the front door as we approached and said in the suavest voice I'd ever heard, "Miss Pinkey, your mother has requested your presence in the library."

Hailey Joanne rolled her eyes and sighed. "Oh, all right. Mango, you wait here. I want to be with you when you see my room."

The butler led Hailey Joanne to the library. Left alone, I was in awe of the size of the . . . what should I call it? It was definitely more than a hallway. . . . It was a lobby, like in a hotel. At the far end was a curved double staircase, the kind that looked like arms open to hug you. At the top of the long flight of stairs was a balcony that seemed to float over the lobby.

I turned to look at the huge portraits on the walls around me. There was an imposing painting of a man I recognized as Hailey Joanne's father, Max Pinkey, from his TV commercials for his limousine service and car dealership. Beside his portrait was a full-length oil painting of a stunning woman in a shimmering gown with a train of ostrich feathers. The sparkle in her eyes matched the diamond earrings and necklace she wore. She had a long neck that made me think of elegance and swans. I was so dazzled by the portrait that I had to blink a few times before I could pull myself away.

Across the room was another even larger portrait that made me take a step back. Looming high above me was an intimidating, silver-haired, dark-skinned woman whose lips turned down at the corners, and her eyes stared out as if she was daring me to ask her to smile. I was a bit startled when a silky voice came up behind me.

"That's my grandmother, Irma Beth Trueheart." I turned around and faced the glamorous woman from the full-length portrait. "She founded a line of haircare products for black women and became a millionaire before she was twenty-five.

123

She married my grandfather, Doctor August Trueheart"— she pointed to another commanding portrait at the top of the stairs of a distinguished, light-complexioned black man— "and together they led the charge to integrate all the public schools and hospitals in our state."

Now I understood why Hailey Joanne went to Trueheart Middle School; it was named after her great-grandparents. She was what they called a legacy. Funny—she never bragged about that. If my great-grandparents were famous civil rights activists who had a school named for them, I would be so proud. I'd have let everybody know.

"Thanks for the history lesson, Mother." Hailey Joanne walked into the room and sighed impatiently. "May we go to my room now? Tessica is waiting with the dresses."

Mrs. Pinkey's eyes darted toward her daughter with a sting of irritation, but her lips still smiled. "You may find your way to your room after you've reacquainted yourself with your manners. Introduce your friend."

For the first time in my life, I actually saw Hailey Joanne back down. With her tail between her legs, she moved next to me and very formally said, "Mother, I'd like to present my best friend, Mango Delight Fuller. Mango, this is my mother, Altovese Trueheart-Pinkey."

Staggered to be introduced as her "best friend" I actually gulped as Mrs. Trueheart-Pinkey reached out her diamond ring–studded hand. I said, "Pleased to meet you, Mrs. Pinkey," and—I can't believe it—I actually curtsied for the first time in my life.

My attempt at a curtsey was a little wobbly, but I guess it was okay because Mrs. Pinkey said, "Charming. You are such a charming young girl. No wonder they named you *Delight*. Would you mind if I referred to you by your middle name?"

"No, ma'am, I wouldn't mind at all."

She moved in closer, and I was kind of bewildered when she reached out and ran her diamond-clad fingers through my Afro puff. "Nice, healthy, thick hair. Outstanding. We have a product line called Silky Siren that would relax your hair and lengthen it . . . down to below your shoulder blades. Would you like to try it? We have plenty of samples in the basement salon."

"That's very kind of you, ma'am, but my mom won't let me use chemical relaxers in my hair."

"Don't tell me—she wears an Afro?"

"No. Uh. Dreadlocks."

Mrs. Pinkey's diamond-clad fingers landed on the collar of her blouse, her head tilted back, and she took a breath as though she were counting to ten before saying anything that might appear offensive. "Well. To each her own. *N'est-ce pas?*"

As she headed back to the library, she fluttered her fingers just like Hailey Joanne and said, "I look forward to seeing you again very soon, Delight."

As her mother disappeared down the corridor, Hailey

Joanne whispered, "She so pisses me off. Do you know why she called me into the library?"

"No. . . ."

"Last Friday, I told her I didn't want Minelli's to cater my birthday party because Brooklyn is such a *B*, and I *don't* mean the first letter in her name. She went out and got a phone that was better than mine after I helped her pick out her first phone, the one you destroyed. I know she did that on purpose so she could act like she was better than me. Then she got an attitude when I told her I posted your audition on YouTube. She was planning on posting it if you'd flopped, but you were great, and she didn't want anyone to see that. Have you ever heard of anyone so mean? I mean, we should be proud of you! *Then* she goes and transfers to Islington. I know she did that just so she can race against me in the GOT 5K. Have you ever heard of anything so petty and super competitive?"

Before I could answer her, Hailey Joanne pointed at the curved staircase to the right. "You go over there. I'll race you to the top." The second I got to the staircase, she shouted, "Go!" Up we went, as fast as we could go. Because of my long legs, I could take three steps at a time, but something told me to chill out—winning a race had started all my troubles in the first place. So, I'm not saying I lost on purpose, but I was fine with Hailey Joanne reaching the landing just a hair before me.

We leaned against the iron rail of the balcony catching

our breath when Hailey Joanne bit her lower lip and said, "I had another reason for posting your tryout on YouTube."

"You did?"

"Yes. I did it as a thank-you."

"Thank me? For what?"

"For not ratting us out. If you had told Lipschultz that Brooklyn and I had hidden our phones in the wastebasket, I would have been in trouble, too, because I lied about not having my phone with me. Brooklyn just couldn't appreciate that you weren't a snitch and didn't tell the whole truth. But I did, because Mother would have taken away my phone for a month if she ever found out I dared to break a rule in my great-grandparents' school. So, when you got up there at the audition and sang your buns off, I posted it as a way of, I don't know, showing I thought you were über crisp."

"Wow, I had no idea." It was strange, but to my eyes, at that moment, Hailey Joanne advanced from being a paper cutout doll to a life-size mannequin.

She gripped my hand and led me down a long corridor. "So, anyhow, when I told Mother I didn't want Minelli's to cater my party, Mother said, 'No, no, no, it's too late to hire a new caterer. You'll just have to get over yourself, Hailey Joanne.' Can you believe that? I hope she doesn't think I'm going to invite Brooklyn to my party just because her father is catering. If she does come, she can just stay in the back with the help." She started to giggle. "Actually, it would be fun if they put her in one of those waiter costumes and made her serve."

This was my chance to fulfill my mission—the perfect set up. If I could have spoken up right then, not only might I have been able to secure the catering job for Dada, but I'd also have saved the day for Hailey Joanne. But just as I was about to speak, she opened the double doors to her bedroom, and I almost swallowed my tongue, teeth, and lips.

CHAPTER 13

Faking Friends

You know that scene in *The Wizard of Oz* when Dorothy steps out of her old black-and-white house and everything around her is in color? That's how I felt stepping into Hailey Joanne's bedroom. I'd never seen a room like that, not even in the movies. It was filled with light. The pink-and-silver pattern on the wallpaper made the whole room glisten. We removed our shoes at the door, because the carpet was long, fluffy, and white, like an Angora cat. (That's right, a white carpet in a kid's room!) Her bed was circular, up on a platform, and surrounded by a cloud of pink sheer curtains. All of the furniture was mirrored, which made the ginormous room look even ginormouser. I knew *ginormouser* wasn't a word, but a room like that deserves its own language.

"Outstanding! I love it," Hailey Joanne cheered, clapping her hands and spinning around herself. "I love to see the looks on girls' faces when they first walk into my room. Pretty spectac, huh?"

I nodded. "It sure is."

"Father had it duplicated from a real princess's boudoir he saw in Dubai. Come on, my stylist is meeting us in my dressing room."

I followed her through frosted-glass double doors into a dressing room almost as large as the bedroom and really fancy. Floor-to-ceiling mirrors lined all the walls except for the glass showcase closets holding legions of dresses, pants, blouses, sweaters, shoes, handbags—enough clothing and accessories to fill two or three boutiques. There were pink velvet chairs, a pink carpet, and a pink crystal chandelier hanging from the domed ceiling. I felt like I was inside a jewelry box.

I was feeling light-headed. Surrounded by so much luxury, I was about to hyperventilate when I noticed, standing alongside a clothing rack, a tall, X-ray-thin woman wearing an outfit that would have looked better on her granddaughter. This was Tessica, the stylist. She zipped across the room and air-kissed Hailey Joanne while leading her to a rack of garment bags. I was so completely ignored that I checked my reflection in the surrounding mirrors to make sure I was actually there.

Tessica unzipped dress bags to display full-length gowns, shimmering pantsuits, and cocktail dresses. These were the kinds of clothes movie stars wore on red carpets. Hailey Joanne, finger on her chin, perused the collection very casually. If she wrinkled her nose and shook her head, Tessica pushed the dress away and moved on to the next. If Hailey Joanne moved her head from side to side and shrugged, Tessica pulled out that outfit and hung it on another rack that I assumed was for the clothes Hailey Joanne would eventually try on.

Tessica displayed a high-collared, sleeveless, red mini-dress covered in bugle beads. "Vintage Halston, cupcake," she said in a voice that sounded like it got stuck in a blender set to "chop." "It doesn't get any better than this!"

Hailey Joanne gasped, hand over her mouth. "Mango would look fabulous in this!"

The stylist frowned, making her wrinkles all the more prominent. "Mango? Who's that?"

When Hailey Joanne pointed to me. Tessica acted as if she hadn't even known I was in the room. "Oh, you! Are you looking to buy a dress, too?"

"Um. Not exactly."

"Of course you are," Hailey Joanne said, taking the dress from Tessica and heading toward me. "You're the star of our school play; you have to dress the part." Gripping my arm, she led me to what turned out to be a mirrored door to a dressing room and scooted me in. "Try it on. It'll look fabulous with those long legs of yours."

She closed the door before I could protest, and there I was, surrounded by four floor-to-ceiling mirrors and about ten thousand reflections of myself. The dress was very heavy but so, so, so beautiful. It was lined with satin and was sewn so perfectly it took me a while before I found the zipper along the side. What could it hurt to try it on? Just because I tried it on didn't mean I'd have to buy it.

I hustled out of my jeans and T-shirt and slid into the dress. It was amazing. The lining felt like a cool breeze against my skin. I turned this way and that, admiring myself in the mirror. I sucked in my cheeks and struck poses the way actresses and models do on a red carpet. No wonder they all looked so confident and beautiful; wearing a dress like this, or even just trying it on, made you feel like a zillion bucks. I was losing myself in a fantasy of flashing lights, surrounded by photographers calling out my name. "Mango, over here!" "Hey, Mango, give us a smile, darling?" "Oh, yes, perfect!" The next day my picture would be all over the society and gossip blogs, and I'd be trending on all the fashion websites.

My reverie was interrupted by a knock at the door. It was Tessica. "Mango? Come on out, biscuit, if you're dressed."

Mango? Biscuit? Seriously? Was she trying to diss me? She probably couldn't hear very well, what with her advanced age and all the rattling bangles she wore on her stick arms. I opened the door and stepped out. Tessica guided me to the center of the room, and then walked around me as if appraising a piece of furniture in a showroom. "Amazing. It's as if it were designed and altered to fit you perfectly. Is it too heavy?"

"Not really. I mean, it felt heavier when I was holding it, but now that it's on—"

"That's the sign of a great designer. You must buy this dress!"

Another door opened, and Hailey Joanne stepped out of her dressing room wearing a peach-colored, sequined dress that fit her like a second skin. She was very well developed for her age, or *any* age, with the kind of figure that made girls lime-green with envy. The way that dress showed off her shape let girls like me know that there was no competition when it came to who the reigning queen of the school was. It seemed as though we were mirroring each other the way both our mouths dropped open when we saw one another.

"Outstanding!" Hailey Joanne exclaimed.

"Me? You! You look like . . . like . . . some kind of mermaid princess." We grabbed each other's hands and shimmied in our glittering couture.

Hailey Joanne said, "Mango, you just have to wear that dress to my party."

I let go of her hand and stepped back as all of the air whizzed out of the room. "I can't. There is no way I can afford this."

Tessica wrinkled her brow to the point that she looked like the parchment the Declaration of Independence was written on. "Why not? Why did you come to a private showing if you're concerned about money?"

"Tessica!" Hailey Joanne scolded. "I invited her. She's my best friend. Her family doesn't . . . well, her father has a restaurant or something, but they're not rich."

Tessica's eyes narrowed. "Which restaurant does your father own? Have I heard of it? Have I been there?" She was examining me closely, and I felt like an ant caught under a magnifying glass in the blazing sun. I was afraid my armpits would start to sweat at any minute and ruin the satin lining of the dress.

Still, I didn't want to lie, so I decided to clear things up. "My father doesn't own a restaurant. He is a chef. At least he was until he lost his job recently. Now he's a caterer."

Hailey Joanne's perfectly plucked eyebrows arched. "A caterer? Really? Is he booked? Would he be too busy to do my party?"

I couldn't believe she was asking me what I had come to ask her. I was beginning to hyperventilate again and felt a trickle of sweat under my armpit.

Hailey Joanne moved nose to nose with me and said, "Listen, if you can get your father to cancel whatever else he is booked to do and cater my party, I will see to it that you get to wear this dress."

"What? Really?"

She held up her right hand and said, "Pinkey swear!" Normally when someone says "pinky swear," you twist your two pinkies together to seal the deal, but when I held my pinky up, Hailey Joanne looked at me as if I were odd. So I dropped my pinky and then realized she said it because her *name* was Pinkey.

"Well, I guess I can call home and ask him."

"Right now. Do it right now!"

Hailey Joanne started to drag me out of the room, but Tessica stopped her and made us change out of the dresses before we left her sight. Everything after that was sort of a blur, but one thing was clear: after a phone interview with Mrs. Pinkey (she remembered Dada from the great job he did catering her anniversary when he worked at Minelli's), he got the job catering the birthday party. I had the contract in my backpack. I was a hero. And I would get to wear that amazing red, beaded, vintage Halston dress to the party. Maybe faking friends with Hailey Joanne wouldn't turn out to be so bad after all.

CHAPTER 14

The Kissing Game

For the next two weeks, I was a golden child who could do no wrong—a ray of sunshine to my folks. Mom was hyped that I had arranged for Dada to get this opportunity all on my own. She was sure it would lead him and the family to the next stage in our lives. Every time I walked into a room, Mom's lips would peel back in a bright smile. She didn't even give her usual stern lecture when I got a *C* on my Anne Frank book report. Instead, she said, "I understand that you're very busy with learning lines, songs, and dances for the play, so we'll overlook this one, okay?" I gladly agreed but was disappointed that I hadn't done a better job, because I really felt for Anne Frank and all she went through.

Rehearsal for the play was going . . . well, I guess I could say it was going okay. The songs were great and fun to sing. I was learning so much from Mr. Ramsey about singing from my diaphragm, breath control, warming up properly, not making bad habits that strain the vocal cords, and keeping my eyes open when I sang. I was becoming more and more confident as a performer, and for the first time, singing was more than something fun I could do. The more I learned about singing properly, the harder I worked to do it better.

The not-so-great part was my acting. Playing a character, pretending to be someone other than myself, that was a real challenge. I was no actress. And although TJ was as nice as he could be, I was embarrassed when I had to say romantical things to him, and I still couldn't bring myself to kiss him. Or let him kiss me.

In *Yo, Romeo!* our kissing scene was set in a recording studio. I was in the booth recording, and Romeo sneaks in to watch. When everyone takes a break, my agent (aka Izzy) sneaks Romeo into the booth with me, and we sing "Duet Forever" to each other as we fall in love. At the end of the scene, we kiss. The first few times we just mimed kissing from a distance. But during the fifth week, Bob wanted us to do the scene for real and go all the way through with the kiss.

Before I was called to run the scene, I went to the bathroom, swooshed water around in my mouth, and chewed a handful of breath mints. When it was time to rehearse, my breath was immaculate, so I thought I was ready. So did Izzy . . . and the rest of the cast. *Everyone* had gathered around to watch. My hands were shaking. Bob caught on and told Boss Chloe to clear the auditorium. Closed rehearsal.

I calmed down a little bit. Bob walked me to the wings on the side of the stage and said, "You're doing great, Mango, but you have to stop trying to separate yourself from Juliet. You are her, and she is you. Trust it and let yourself go."

I whispered, "But I'm scared."

"Great. It's perfectly fine to be scared. Juliet is scared, too. Romeo is her first love, and this is the first time she's ever kissed a boy. She is feeling just what you are feeling. Go with it and let yourself play the scene."

Bob was right. My character was feeling shy, scared, embarrassed, and nervous—just like me. I went back onstage. Mr. Ramsey, at the piano, played, and TJ and I sang. Trusting that my feelings were Juliet's feelings opened me up. I sang the same notes as before, but my feelings were free, and so my voice took off like never before. I could see in TJ's face that he could tell something in me was different, real, and true.

The song ended, and we moved in for a kiss. His head tilted one way, and I tilted mine the other way. Just before our lips touched, I covered my mouth with my hand, and TJ wound up kissing my knuckles.

Bob's frustration with me finally got the better of him. He pulled on his cockatoo hair and growled as he stormed out of the auditorium. Mr. Ramsey, blinking furiously, said, "Uh . . . just hang tight, you two. I'll be right back." He hurried up the aisle after Bob.

TJ and I were alone. I could hear my heart *thump thumping* in my chest. Snippets of conversation, laughter, and kids running lines seeped in from the hallway where the other cast members were waiting. The empty auditorium seats in their upright positions seemed to be frowning and judging me.

I looked in TJ's direction, mumbled "Sorry," and then turned and walked upstage, facing away from the judgmental seats and away from TJ. The only one I couldn't get away from was myself and how lame I was. Why had I ever agreed to do this?

Ego—that's what it was. Bob had stroked my ego, and I'd gone along with it even though I knew deep down inside that I didn't have an ounce of what it took to play a character. I could smell the mildew of shame oozing from every pore.

I heard TJ's footsteps on the wooden floor behind me. His biker boots. They made such a clunky sound. He got close enough for me to hear him breathing. For about a minute he was silent, and then all of a sudden he blurted out, "A sloth takes a whole month to travel a single mile."

I turned to face him. "Huh?"

"Nothing."

"No, it's not nothing. Why do you always come out with this weird stuff? Do you think I'm a . . . are you calling me a sloth?"

"No. Uh-uh. No way." He kind of snickered and stepped back. "It's just that . . . I don't know. I'm weird, I guess. I mean, I know a lot of obscure facts. I was a real nerdball when I was a kid. Read the *Guinness World Records* books and stuff like that from cover to cover about twenty times."

"So why do you keep . . . ?"

"I can't help it. Weird facts pop into my head, and I just blurt them out when I get nervous."

I smiled. "Why would you get nervous around me?"

"Because." He looked down at his boots. "I always get nervous before performing with my band. Or when I'm about to play them a new song I wrote. And when I'm around a girl I like."

O!

M!

G!

Z ! ! !

A part of me wanted to leap into the air and pump my fists. Another part of me wanted to run away. And the biggest part of me wanted to pee. But I stayed right where I was, ignoring my bladder and trying not to look away from him. He lifted his head and I could see in his kiwi-green eyes that he was sincere. I just knew it. I couldn't help it, I looked away. I couldn't think of anything to say, even though I knew I liked him, too. I thought maybe I should just say that, so I swallowed, took a deep breath and . . .

But before I could say anything, he started singing "Duet Forever." The love song. He started singing it without the music. You know, a cappella. He sounded great. I joined in. He reached for my hand. I reached for his. We sang the entire song that way, just looking at each other. When the song ended, he leaned in toward me, I mirrored him. His head tilted, my head tilted, too, and . . .

"Seriously! No. Really? You mean it! Call the ambulance, I'm gonna have a heart attack!" Izzy slammed her ample body against the door of a parked car, and the alarm went off. We were both so shocked, we ran down the street screaming and laughing. We finally stopped on the next block. Izzy looked back to where the car was still whooping. "Holy heart attack." She crossed herself. "You think the police are after us?"

She was so dramatic, but I couldn't help but laugh.

"Quit laughing and tell me about the kiss before I'm carted off to jail."

"Calm down. It wasn't really a kiss. It was more like a peck."

"A peck on the cheek or a peck on the lips?"

Heat rose to my face. "On the lips."

Izzy started yelping again. "That is *so* trending worldwide!"

I grabbed her hand, and we continued walking home. "Listen, keep this to yourself, okay? The last place I want to be trending is all over the school."

"Of course. The news of your first kiss will never cross my lips."

That made me think. Was it really *my* first kiss? Or was it my character Juliet's first kiss? Or both? I know TJ said he liked me, but did he really *like* like me or was he just trying to get me to play the full scene?

I began to question why every time something good happened to me, my insecurity would find a crack in my happiness and drip, drip, drip inside like water until the happiness was washed away.

As I was saying goodbye to Izzy, she grabbed me in a bear hug and whispered in my ear, "Welcome to the First Kiss Club, Mango!" Walking the rest of the way home, I wondered if I looked different, if Mom and Dada would be able to tell that I had passed a life milestone today. I slowed down, trying to catch a glimpse of my reflection in the windows of parked cars, but decided that looked kind of sociopath-vain, so I just picked up my pace on the rest of the way home, imagining a lavender aura glowing all around me.

CHAPTER 15

Good Taste

Mom was too busy to notice that I'd had a life-changing experience. She, Jasper, and his diaper bag were on their way out when I arrived.

"Where are you going?"

"Oh, hi, Mango. I was waiting for you to get back and take care of Jasper, but I'm in a hurry."

"Why?"

"Your father is about to have a tasting for the party menu. He wants me to sample everything before the Pinkeys arrive."

"Oh, can I go, too?"

"Do you have a lot of homework? We may be there for a while."

"I can do most of it in the car. Don't worry, I'll get it done. Please say yes."

"All right. Come on. We have to leave right away."

I was so excited. Dada had rented a commercial kitchen to prepare the food for Hailey Joanne's birthday party.

Caterers had to use restaurants or commercial kitchens when preparing food for the public. It was the law in our city. Luckily Dada had included the cost of renting the space into his fee, so he was still going to make a healthy profit from the party. Almost five thousand dollars!

The commercial kitchen was large and super-clean. It had the same kind of cooking equipment we had in our at home, but there was more of everything, and everything was bigger.

Dada and his assistant had laid out trays of hors d'oeuvres, yummy cake samples, colorful non-alcoholic drinks, and slices of twelve varieties of pizza. He gave me a hug when I entered the space, looked into my eyes, and said, "Hey, baby, what's that sparkle in your eye?"

"Sparkle? I don't know what you're talking about." Had he actually seen a difference in me? A new glow? A maturity? A twinkle that said, "Yes, your baby girl *kissed* a boy!"

Before I was able to find out what he meant by *sparkle*, Mom insisted we start tasting, because the Pinkeys would arrive any minute.

I loved the shrimp, cheese, scallion, salami, and asparagus canapés, but the anchovies made me want to barf, and I suggested Dada eighty-six those. He did. The salmon-and-shrimp phyllo purses were yummy, but my favorites were the jerk-beef sliders and the pan-fried pâtés, made with chicken livers, bacon, spinach, and garlic. I knew I didn't have the same tastes as an ordinary girl my age, but I'd been living with a chef my entire life, and my palette had been exposed to all sorts of flavors since the day I started solid foods.

All the pizzas and cakes were wonderful, so I couldn't choose which ones I thought the Pinkeys would like best. But while Mom thought the ginger ale and tropical fruit punch were the most appropriate beverages, I assured Dada that his homemade blueberry soda would win the day. Number one: it was delicious. Number two: no one had ever had soda made out of blueberries before. And number three: Hailey Joanne would want to serve something unique so her party would stand out above and beyond any birthday party for years.

The Pinkeys arrived in a flurry of air-kisses. I noticed Mrs. Pinkey observing my mom's dreadlocks (which she was wearing in a stylish French roll) very closely but pretending she wasn't looking at them at all. Mr. Pinkey strode over to Dada and gave him—what I could tell from Dada's wince—a bone-crushing handshake. Hailey Joanne was noticeably subdued in the presence of her parents, but when they weren't around, she stepped into her mother's place as the queen of all she surveyed.

The tasting was going great. Hailey Joanne skipped all of the hors d'oeuvres except for the jerk-beef sliders. I prodded her into trying one, and she loved it. She concentrated on the pizzas and the cakes, insisting that I try each one along with her, although I explained that I had already tasted them. I was getting very full as we went along, but I kept taking bite after bite after bite because Hailey Joanne wanted me to, and she might think that I thought the food wasn't good if I didn't.

I could tell that she really liked the food, because she kept closing her eyes, savoring every bite. She kept thanking me for Dada and saying, "The secret to a great party is great food, and this food is spectac! My party is going to be one for the history books thanks to you." I felt such a rush of warm feelings toward Hailey Joanne. Who was this girl, and why had I never seen this side of her before? Was it my fault? Had I been in the wrong about her all along?

After we'd tasted almost everything and our parents were finalizing the menu, Hailey Joanne pulled me aside with "The most exciting news ever!"

"What is it?" I asked.

"I've hired an iconic band for my party. You'll never guess who. Try. Go on. Try to guess!"

"Uh, Maroon 5?"

"Huh? You're not trying hard enough."

I thought of all the groups on the pop charts. Her family would be able to afford entertainment like that. I mean, she did have Gabriel Faust at her last birthday party, why should this one be any different?

"Oh, all right, you're taking too long—I'll tell you. I've hired the Halfrican Americans!"

The Halfrican Americans weren't famous anywhere

except at our school and around the community. "TJ's band? That's who you hired?"

"Yes! I love them. And that TJ, OMGZ, he's is so cute in a crazy, weird kind of way. I think he likes me, but that's not why I hired them."

Chunks of my heart crumbled and landed in my stomach amongst the canapés, pizzas, and cakes. Nausea wrapped its arms around my torso and began to sway me from side to side as Hailey Joanne kept on talking. "He played a couple of the songs from *Yo, Romeo!* for me, and I was wishing you and TJ would sing a few of them at the party." She grabbed my hands and squeezed hard, using the grip she probably inherited from her father. "Please say yes! Pretty please. It would be your birthday gift to me. Please!"

"Yes. Yes, of course." I slid my fingers from her grip. "I didn't know you liked TJ."

"I've always liked him from afar. You know how it is with a boy you *really* like. Those are the ones you can't really talk to or flirt with or be yourself around. But now that he's in the play and you're in the play, he couldn't say no when I told him how much you wanted to sing with him at the party."

"When did you tell him that?"

"Last night. We were texting back and forth for over an hour before I finally convinced him. Aren't you happy about it?"

I couldn't risk angering Hailey Joanne, not after my dada

spent all this money to rent a kitchen and make all of this sample food. So I said, "Of course I'm happy. I'm beyond!"

She looked at me suspiciously. "So why don't you tell your face?"

I realized my expression was showing my real confusion and heartbreak, so I plastered on a bright smile as fast as I could. "Seriously, I'm . . . I'm delighted, just a little full. You know how sleepy you get just after you've eaten a lot of great food!"

"Oh, Mango, you're the best. You know the girls on my squad, the other Cell-belles, I could never tell them anything like this."

"Why not?"

"I don't know. . . . Maybe it's because I have to act differently around them. They treat me like I'm their leader or something. If they knew my real feelings, they would make fun of me for liking TJ, because, well . . . he's not the type of society boy my parents or my friends would expect me to go for. Of course, they'd text about it behind my back so I wouldn't see it." She bit her lip and stared at me for a couple of seconds. "But you're different, Mango. I can be myself around you. You get me. You know what I mean?"

It took me a moment before I realized I was holding my breath. I mean, in the last minute, I found out she liked the same boy I liked and on top of that she really liked being my friend. She trusted me, she wasn't faking at all, and she was being really nice! So, I couldn't help it—I just blurted out the most fake thing I've ever said: "Yeah. You get me, too!"

Hailey Joanne leaned in and air-kissed both my cheeks. "Listen, I'm having my glam squad—a hairstylist, manicurist, masseuse, and makeup artist—come to my house on the day of the party, and I want you to come, too. We'll have a spa day and get all dolled up and roll up to the party together. Say you'll come! After all, that's where your fabulous dress will be." She grabbed my hands and squeezed them again. "Say yes. I can't even hear the word *no*. When it comes to my birthday, *no* is not in my vocabulary."

Deep down I wanted to say no, because it wouldn't be fair to keep faking with her when she was inviting me because she thought we were becoming real friends. I didn't want to turn her down, not after what she just said. If I turned her down and hurt her feelings, she might have changed her mind about Dada. So I flashed the brightest smile I could and said, "Yes, sure, of course I'll come. I've never had a glam squad before. This'll be über crisp!"

Watching the Pinkeys leave, my feelings tumbled all over each other. Should I be mad at TJ for playing at the party of a girl who had a crush on him? Did he know she had a crush? Did he kiss me because he liked me, or was it just rehearsal for him? Would I really have told Hailey Joanne yes if I weren't afraid of ruining everything for Dada?

Besides, she was becoming a real person to me—not just some queen diva I could use to get what I wanted. Faking a friendship with her was becoming harder and harder, because she actually believed me. I was beginning to get a headache. I closed my eyes, shook my head to reset my brain, and decided I wouldn't think about it any more . . . at least, not until I was at home in my bed.

Dada and Mom were bubbling as they put all the food away and cleaned the kitchen. I realized I hadn't seen the two of them this happy together since Jasper was born. They were joking and laughing and kind of bumping into each other on purpose. Yep, I believe they were actually flirting.

I sat by the door with Jasper asleep in his car seat. He looked so sweet and innocent. Must be nice to be a baby with no worries except who is going to feed you and change your diapers. As he got older, like me, the worries and responsibilities would pile on. And he would have to make choices to let go of things he might really want if it's for the good of the whole family.

As we walked to the car, Dada put his arms around me and said, "The Pinkeys gave me *carte blanche* and a limitless budget. I can buy the best of the best ingredients and do pretty much whatever I want. The most influential people in town are going to be at this party eating my food. This could make my name as a caterer, and I owe it all to you, Mango."

Well, that did it. I had to wipe TJ's kiss and what he had said to me from my memory. I had to erase the newly human Hailey Joanne from my emotional hard drive. It wasn't going to be easy, but I had to put my feelings aside for the good of Dada and my family.

I know this is super weird, but on the ride home, sitting in the back of the car next to Jasper in his car seat, I suddenly got the urge to call Brooklyn Minelli. Yep, that's right: the only person I could think of sharing my feelings and confusions with was "she who must not be named."

With everything going on with the play and TJ, and trying to get the catering job for Dada, and suddenly being Hailey Joanne's "instant bestie," I had kind of blocked Brooklyn from my mind. But I had to admit: every so often she would seep through the tiny cracks in the wall of distractions I'd built against her, and I'd miss my ex-bestie. Yeah, she did me major wrong, but we'd had a lot of fun together before that. And right then, she was the only person I could think of that I could talk about my deepest, most secret feelings with.

As soon as we got home, I picked up the cordless phone, headed to my room, and began punching in Brooklyn's home phone number. Just as I got to the last digit—

Whoa! Hold up! What was I thinking? Brooklyn had already betrayed me once. Who's to say she wouldn't do it again? If I called her and told her about what was going on between me, Hailey Joanne, and TJ, who's to say she wouldn't text Hailey Joanne with everything I told her just to sabotage my life again? And since Hailey Joanne was morphing into a real person, I started to wonder why I hadn't seen who she really was in the first place. Was it because she and Brook were rivals and because I was so close to Brook that I could only see Hailey Joanne through her eyes?

No, I would never let myself get brainwashed that way again. No way. There was no one I could trust with everything going on inside me right now. I'd just have to deal with my feelings on my own. I clicked the phone off and sat on my bed.

Then Izzy popped into my head. Maybe I should call her? We were becoming really good friends, but . . . I wasn't sure. I confided private things to Brook really early into our friendship, and look what happened. No—even though I really liked Izzy and how our friendship was growing, I decided to take my time before going all in with any friend ever again. All of a sudden, I felt cold and clammy, and a chill rattled my rib cage.

It was loneliness wrapping its skeleton arms around me.

CHAPTER 16

Triangle Crush

There was nothing more important than Dada catering Hailey Joanne's party. His future was riding on this, and since my falling out with Brooklyn was the reason he got fired in the first place, it was up to me to do whatever I could to make things right. Task number one: keep Hailey Joanne from having a meltdown and calling off the party or firing Dada. She was the kind of girl used to getting what she wanted, and for the next week, all she could talk about was how much she wanted TJ to be her boyfriend. Task number two: Discourage TJ from liking me and myself from liking him.

The next time I saw TJ was at rehearsal. I was sitting in the auditorium going over my lines when he came in and sat next to me. I looked over, and he gave me the sweetest, shyest smile ever. "Hi, Mango."

It took everything I had not to return his smile. I simply said, "Hi."

He leaned in. "How are you?"

I looked at him with the most annoyed expression I could make and said, "I'm studying my lines now, if you don't mind."

His smile melted away. "Okay. Sure. Didn't mean to bother you." He got up and walked off. I put my head down, my eyes focused on my script. It felt as if my guts were being twisted into a loom bracelet. What I had just done was cruel. I had never been cruel to anyone on purpose, and it felt horrible. But I owed it to Dada; I couldn't mess this up for him or my family.

I kept my distance whenever TJ was around. I only spoke to him when I was playing Juliet. I did my best to avoid looking into his kiwi-green eyes. When we rehearsed the kissing scene, I just gave him a quick peck automatically, like a robot. As soon as it was over, I walked away.

Izzy kept pumping me for "relationship" updates. I told her there was no relationship. I didn't like him in that way, and he didn't like me.

"But you told me you liked him."

"I said that I like him, yeah, but that doesn't mean that I *like* like him."

"Well, okay, right, but you did say that he said that he *like* liked you, right?"

"Right. But just because a boy *like* likes a girl doesn't mean she has to *like* like him back. Right?" I was lying to myself, and I was lying to my friend, but I had a duty to my family.

On the way home, I made Izzy promise not to talk about TJ. She said, "Okay, okay, subject dropped. You don't have to tell me twice. Moving on. So, let's talk about the party on Saturday. What time should I be at your house?"

"My house?"

"Yeah, I'm your plus one. We have to arrive together. My mom said she'd drive us. So what time should I pick you up?"

Uh-oh. With all the drama going on, I forgot to tell Izzy about Hailey Joanne and the glam squad. When I filled her in on where I would be on Saturday, she completely deflated, like a hot-air balloon with the gas turned off.

"I guess I'm not invited to the spa day, huh?"

"I don't think so. I could ask if you really want me to."

"Never mind, Mango. If you really wanted me there, you would have asked from the get-go." Izzy bit her lower lip and looked as though she were going to cry. Not the kind of crying she did to warm up her voice, but a really sad cry, because she was hurt and I was to blame.

I put my arm around her. "Listen, Izzy, there is so much going on that I can't explain to you now. I mean, I never even wanted to go to the party, but my dad got the catering job, and if I back out . . . you see, I have to do what Hailey Joanne wants, so. . . ."

Izzy removed my arm from her shoulder. "So you're being fake friends with her so your dad keeps the job?"

"In a way, I guess . . ."

"And you're being fake friends with me, so I can help you with the play?"

"No!"

155

"How do I know that? How do you even know if you're being real when you spend so much time being fake? Seriously, you need to check yourself."

I was shocked into silence. I hate to admit it, but Izzy was right. I was fake-friending Hailey Joanne and fake-unfriending TJ. I did get close to Izzy again because of the play—but that wasn't the only reason, was it?

When we got to Izzy's house, I said, "Don't worry, I'll work everything out about the party."

She said, "Forget about it. I don't want to go anymore."

"You have to go. I don't want to be there without you. You're the one who accepted the invitation in the first place." I held her hands in mine and squeezed them really tight, the way Hailey Joanne did when she wanted to make a point. "If there is one thing I know, Isabel Otero, is that you and I are *not* fake friends. From kinder to the ender, remember?"

Izzy sort of smiled and nodded and then looked down and wouldn't make eye contact with me. I remembered how I felt when my friendship with Brooklyn was first starting to fall apart. How confused I was. How hurt. I didn't want to let Izzy walk away feeling like that. I had to make things right. I bent down to find her eyes and make sure she could see mine. "I owe you so much, Izzy. You are a major reason for all the good things that have been happening to me lately. You gave me confidence. You shared your circle of friends with me when I was all alone after Brooklyn dumped me. I could never ever fake-friend you. Please say you believe me."

She smiled, and the twinkle in her eyes returned when she looked at me. "Okay, I believe you. I really do."

We hugged it out, and I said, "I'll see to it your name is on the list, and I'll even give you my invitation. I won't need one if I'm walking through the door with the birthday girl. And once I get inside, I'm heading straight for you. Promise."

"Okay. I guess I'll go. Where else am I going to wear a dress made out of balloons?"

"Balloons?!"

"Well, not really, but that's what the fabric feels like. Mamí is making it for me. It's really colorful, but it's not my first choice. Between us, I'm wearing it so I won't hurt her feelings."

"You mean you're fake-liking it?"

Izzy laughed. "Okay. You got me! I guess we all have to fake it sometimes." We laughed and hugged, and I couldn't stop smiling the rest of the way home. Izzy was a true friend because she kept it real with me. I liked that. When I walked in the door, Mom was on the phone saying, "Here she is now. She just got in." She handed me the phone. "It's your best friend!"

Hailey Joanne had declared me her new BFF, and so she called me at home every night to moon over TJ and ask question after question about his every move at rehearsal. "Was he in a good mood? How was his dancing? Has he memorized all his lines? Did you see him talking to any other girls? You'd tell me if you did, wouldn't you? Do you think he likes me? He was looking at me in the cafeteria, did you see that?"

What I actually saw was TJ sneaking a look at me. His secret glances always seemed to coincide with the times I risked a secret glance at him. I knew he was hurt because of how I was treating him. I could tell by the way he moped around. All of our scenes together as Romeo and Juliet fell flat. Bob was concerned but kept banking on the hope that we were money players. "I know you two; you're saving your performance for when it counts. When the butts are in the seats and all of our reputations are on the line."

The Friday before the big birthday party was crazy. We couldn't work on the stage, because the sets were being put up, so we had to rehearse in the gymnasium. The floor was taped to the exact dimensions of the set, that way we could do our blocking, but it felt strange to be away from the auditorium.

We were also getting costumes fitted for the first time. There was a steady buzz of excitement in the air as the cast took turns showing off and taking selfies dressed as their characters. My costumes were very flashy because I was playing a pop star. I liked them, but I had a hard time showing it because of what was planned for after.

TJ wanted to rehearse our duet with the Halfrican Americans in his garage before singing at the birthday party. I didn't think we needed to, because all of the band members were in the school orchestra that was playing for the show.

But Hailey Joanne insisted we do the rehearsal—she would be attending and get to spend time with TJ.

She picked me up after rehearsal, and as Mr. Versey drove us to TJ's house, I heard a strange clicking sound. I looked over at Hailey Joanne and noticed the manicured fingernails on each hand rapidly clicking up against one another. I said, "Are you okay, Hailey Joanne?"

She turned toward me, her eyes large and moist. "Do you think he really likes me? I mean, it's really hard for me to tell sometimes and . . . I guess I have to pretend I'm confident so much that I start to believe it, but then again, I really don't know."

A lump started forming in my throat—a cold lump of guilt that instantly made me feel worse for her than I did for myself. I put my hand over her hands to stop the clicking. "I think you should trust your feelings. You've been really nice to him, and look at you, you're beautiful. Why would any boy not like you?"

Hailey Joanne's hands moved on top of mine and squeezed. "You really mean it, Mango?"

I did my best to smile and said, "Yes, I really do." And I kind of sort of did mean it. I mean, she was beautiful. The more I got to know her, the prettier and prettier she became. I was honest about that part of what I said. But I started to wonder: Was it okay to say things you didn't 100 percent mean to spare someone's feelings? Then again, maybe TJ really did *like* like her. I wasn't being very nice to him at all, and she was super kind and super beautiful compared to me.

When Hailey Joanne released my hands from her viselike grip, I had to use all of my resolve not to bring my fingernails to my mouth and start chewing. I hoped this rehearsal would go quickly so I could get home and sort things out by myself.

The band was already jamming when we arrived. Hailey Joanne was in serious fangirl mode, bopping and dancing along to the song they were playing. I couldn't even really hear the music, I had so many heavy thoughts and questions clogging my brain. She nudged me. "What's wrong with you? How can you stand still when they're rocking out like this?"

I shrugged and tried my best to sway to the beat, but my body felt as though it were encased in concrete. Watching Hailey Joanne gush and fawn and flirt with the guy I liked was making my head ache and my eyes burn. She was acting like a rabid groupie, and TJ was actually smiling at her as though he liked her, too. Maybe he did. Maybe the way I was freezing him out made him warm up to Hailey Joanne. I mean, who wouldn't turn to her? She was cute and rich with a *boom-pow* body. Compared to her, I was an unvarnished plank of wood.

When the band finished the song, Hailey Joanne clapped and bounced up and down, proclaiming it her favorite. She insisted they play it more than once at her party.

When it was time for TJ and me to rehearse our duet, Hailey Joanne pulled up a chair and sat so close that it was almost as though she were in the group with us. Talk about *awk*ward. I was supposed to look into TJ's eyes as we sang about falling in love, but I was afraid Hailey Joanne would see that I really liked him, so I sang the entire song looking over his shoulder at the garage door. I don't think Hailey Joanne noticed, because she only had eyes for TJ. But TJ noticed, and when the song was over, he unstrapped his guitar, ripped the cord from the amp, and stomped away.

Hailey Joanne's phone rang, and she stepped out of the garage to get better reception. The band members wandered off to take a break. I just stood in place, looking at my feet, waiting. I could hear Hailey Joanne on the phone outside the garage, arguing with her mother about some party detail. I felt TJ looking at me, but I was afraid that if I looked at him it would reveal how much I liked him and how jealous I was, so I kept my head down.

A low hum was coming from one of the amps. My heart was beating triple-time when TJ said, "Did you know that baby rattlesnakes are—" He stopped talking mid-sentence, cleared his throat, and went on, "What did I do to make you hate me so bad?"

"I don't hate you."

"You sure act like you do. You won't talk to me. You won't look at me. You act like breathing the same air makes you want to puke. If I did something wrong, just say it. Get it out so I can apologize and we can move on."

My throat clenched. Feelings were lining up behind my

tear ducts, trying to push their way out through my eyes. I wanted to beg his forgiveness. Tell him that I still liked him—even more than I had before—but I couldn't. It was too risky.

If Hailey Joanne found out that I liked the boy she liked and he liked me, it would ruin everything for my father.

TJ walked over to me. He reached for my hand, just as I heard Hailey Joanne say, "Whatever, Mother. I really don't care!" She was about to come back into the room, so I snatched my hand away, grabbed my backpack, and told Hailey Joanne I was feeling sick and had to leave right away. She was concerned—she didn't want my illness to upset her party plans. I assured her that it was just nausea, probably something I ate, and I'd be fine the next day.

She hugged me and whispered in my ear as she walked me to the SUV, "If you don't mind, I'll have Versey drive you home. I'm going to stick around and hear TJ play some more songs. And who knows? Maybe I'll get to spend some time alone with him."

As the SUV drove away, I couldn't hold it in. Even though I didn't want to cry, the dam burst and flooded the world with tears.

CHAPTER 17

Party Down-er

Dada had already left for work by the time I flopped out of bed on Saturday, the day of Hailey Joanne's big party. He had hired a couple of line cooks to help prepare the food, and I'm sure they were already prepping and cooking. Mom had arranged for Mrs. Kennedy from the third floor to spend the day with Jasper, because she was going to the commercial kitchen to do whatever Dada needed to make his catering a big success. I showered and got ready to do my part. Hailey Joanne was sending Mr. Versey to pick me up at eleven o'clock so that we could begin our spa day. I was prepared to smile my way through the day, pretending to be her BFBD.

While I was pouring myself a glass of orange juice and noticing the stubby fingernail I had devoured last night, I started thinking about calling Izzy—and the phone rang.

"Hey, girl," Izzy said brightly. "You on your way to get glammed up?"

"OMGZ, I was just thinking about calling you!"

"Happens to me all the time. I've got a sick sense about these things."

"Don't you mean a *sixth* sense?"

"Huh? No, I mean *sick*, like when your friend walks in wearing some fly new boots and you say, 'girl, those boots are sick!' You know? But you mean it in a good way."

"Uh, oh. Okay. . . ."

"So, what's up with you, Mango? What's wrong?"

"What's wrong? What makes you think something is wrong?"

"Like I just said, I've got a sick sense. I can feel it in your voice without even hearing you sing. You've been crying your heart out. Am I right, or am I absolutely, positively right?"

This was truly weird. How could she tell just from the sound of my voice? I hesitated, but then I thought about the other day on the way home and how we sealed our friendship bond outside her house, so . . . I spilled the tea, poured my guts out, laid it all on the line, and released the floodgates. When I finished talking, there was silence.

"Izzy?"

"I'm here."

"You did hear what I just told you, right?"

"Every syllable."

"So . . . what should I do?"

"About?"

"About Hailey Joanne and TJ?"

"Seriously, Mango, you can't do anything about Hailey Joanne or TJ. The only one you can do anything about is you."

That set me back for a second, and I said, "What do you mean?"

"You keep going on and on about how bad you feel about what *you* said, what *you* did, how *you* lied, how *you* were being fake. You never said a thing about what Hailey Joanne did or what TJ did to wrong you. Did you?"

"Uhhhh, no."

"So okay, girl, the only one you have to do something about is you. Figure out how you are you going to make yourself feel better about Mango Delight Fuller."

Dang! Maybe she did have a sick sense or was psychic like her *tía* Maria Magdelena, but she was right. I'd been lying and faking my way through the last few weeks. I thought I had a good reason to do the things I did, but that didn't make it right.

This moment of clarity made me relax, and all at once it was like I could feel my face again. No mask. No fakery. Just me. I smiled and said, "Thanks, Izzy. Thanks for always keeping it one hundred. I have to come clean. I have to tell Hailey Joanne the truth. And I have to do it today."

"Nooooo!" Izzy yelled so loud, I had to move the phone away from my ear. "You can't ruin the poor girl's birthday just to make yourself feel better! That's like a boyfriend telling his girlfriend he's been cheating on her and then saying,

'Wow, now that I've got that off my chest, I feel much better!'
No, please don't tell her today."

"Okay, you're right. But when?"

"Hey, acting is all about timing. When the time is right,
you'll know. But don't wait too long. The longer you wait, the
harder it will be for her to forgive you."

"Thanks, Izzy. What would I do without you?"

"Ha! You don't even want to know. See you at the party!"

When we hung up, I hurried to get dressed. I promised
myself that I'd do my best to make sure Hailey Joanne had
a great birthday, not because of TJ or Dada, but because
she was a cool girl and she deserved it. As soon as I got the
chance, I would come clean and hope she could forgive me.

Hailey Joanne's glam squad was already hard at work
when I arrived and was escorted to the beauty salon in the
basement of the mansion. It looked like the big hair salons
I'd seen downtown with one exception: all of the mirrors were
covered up.

A tall, whippet-thin man with a wild Afro walked up to
me as I gawked at the lack of mirrors and said, "That's right.
No mirrors here, doll. We are magicians, and you don't get to
see the results until the big reveal." He lead me to his station.
"I am Horatio, hairstylist extraordinaire."

Horatio had tattoos of stars, hearts, and hashtags on his
face. They started at the corner of his left eye and trailed
down his cheek and all around his neck. I didn't mean to be

rude, but I couldn't help staring at them. When Horatio saw me looking, I turned away real quick. He said, "Go ahead and look, Miss Girl. That's why I have them. If I didn't want anyone to look, I would never have put a tattoo on this lovely visage." He cackled and snapped his fingers, and his team cackled and snapped along.

Sergio and Tamara were a married couple. He was a makeup artist/manicurist and she was a masseuse/aromatherapist. Tessica was scheduled to arrive later in the afternoon with our dresses. Hailey Joanne was under a hair dryer, flipping through a fashion magazine, and getting a pedicure when I walked over, smiled dutifully, and said, "Happy birthday!"

She thanked me and handed me over to Horatio. "He's going to give you a hair treatment, and when he's finished, you won't recognize yourself."

Horatio took me by the hand and led me to a sink. "First things first, doll: I've got to wash all of whatever you use out of your hair and replenish it with some of Miss Irma Beth Trueheart's magic elixirs. I'm telling you, there ain't nothing in this world better for a black girl's hair than Miss Trueheart's products."

I told him, "My mother doesn't allow me to use chemicals in my hair."

"Oh, honey, your mother won't be opposed to Miss Trueheart's hair care products. They're all-natural and made with essential oils and secret formulas brought by slaves all the way from Africa centuries ago." He paused and put a hand on one hip. "Now do you want a makeover, or not?"

Just imagining Mom's reaction to chemicals in my hair was enough to make me start sweating. But then again, Hailey Joanne had been so nice to invite me to get a makeover from her glam squad. . . . Wouldn't it be rude to turn them down? I was too overwhelmed to say no, so I nodded yes, and the transformation began. He scrubbed my hair like it's never been scrubbed before. Then he applied some kind of goop that I had to let stay on for a half an hour. It began to tingle after a while, so I was relieved when he finally washed it out and set me up under a hairdryer.

The rest of the afternoon flew by. When it was time for my massage, I was a bundle of knots, because my mind was fixed on the phone call with Izzy and what I had to do. But Tamara was such a skilled masseuse, I actually felt relaxed when the massage was over. Sergio gave Hailey Joanne and me skin treatments with mud masks, steam, and "special elixirs" from Miss Trueheart's skin care line. It was uncomfortable when he did a blackhead-extraction treatment on my nose and used a string to shape my eyebrows, but Hailey Joanne kept reminding me, "Beauty has a price, Mango, and the salon is where we pay for it."

Hailey Joanne and I were given brand-new fluffy terrycloth robes to wear while we shared a catered lunch with the glam squad. I had to admit: I was having a good time. Horatio and his crew told hysterical stories about the fashion model divas they'd worked on and the mishaps that had happened on the way to the runway. Hailey Joanne was so funny when she sucked in her cheeks and started doing imitations of how famous models strutted down the runway. Then she pulled me up and we pretended to have a hysterical diva runway-walk battle. We had the glam squad in tears, and we fell on the plush carpet holding our bellies, laughing. I wished the lunch could have gone on all day.

Tessica arrived an hour before we had to leave. We were whisked into private dressing rooms where we put on our dresses and had final touches. Then the glam squad uncovered the mirrors for the big reveal.

I had to do a double take before I recognized myself. My hair fell below my shoulders in soft curls like it never had before. The curls flowed down my back because of the clip-in hair extensions Horatio had added to make me look like a black Rapunzel. The makeup was flawless; I felt like my skin was a canvas and Sergio had created a masterpiece with all of his creams, powders, foundations, and false eyelashes that were so heavy they gave me a sultry, sleepy appearance. With the red, vintage Halston minidress covered in shimmering bugle beads, I actually could have been mistaken for a rock star on her way to the GRAMMYs.

Hailey Joanne was even more dazzling. Her hair, makeup, and dress were all sensational, but the main reason she looked so great was the way she carried herself. Confidence is an accessory I wished the glam squad could have clipped into my hair or brushed on with powder.

Hailey Joanne was accustomed to six-inch high heels, sequins, and all the glamour that came along with them. I tried to copy the way she posed in the mirror as best I could, but next to her gazelle moves, I was a newborn colt stumbling around on knobby legs. Horatio winced when he saw me staggering across the floor as if I were on stilts, so he tried to give me a crash course in walking in high heels. "Keep your knees loose, your head high, your back arched, click your heels three times, and repeat to yourself, 'I am Diana Ross. I *am* Diana Ross!'"

I wasn't sure exactly who Diana Ross was, but I was too afraid to admit it to Horatio; he spoke her name as if she were a goddess. Later in the SUV on the way to the party, Hailey Joanne googled her, and I saw this amazing woman with brown skin and large eyes, like mine. With my makeup and hairstyle, I actually resembled Diana Ross in some of her photos. I smiled at Hailey Joanne and said, "Thank you so much. This has been the best day ever."

Hailey Joanne said, "It's not over yet, Mango. The fun has just begun. Time to turn up!" As we talked and giggled on the way to the party, for the first time I felt like she was my friend—no faking was required.

When we pulled up to the hotel, a line of photographers was snapping pictures of people standing in front of what looked like a room divider. It had the logos of Mr. Pinkey's businesses, pictures of Hailey Joanne, and the words "Happy Birthday" printed all over it. I recognized the mayor and his wife smiling as flashes popped all around them.

Mr. Versey opened the door, and I leaned away as he reached for my hand. Hailey Joanne tried to nudge me on, but I wouldn't budge. "What is that thing? Why are all those photographers there?"

Hailey Joanne touched my shoulder. "Relax, Mango, it's called a step-and-repeat. You stand there and let them take a few pictures of you, and then walk a few steps and do it again until you're off the red carpet. Haven't you seen celebrities do it in magazines or on *Entertainment Tonight*?"

"I've seen them, but I've never done it."

"Trust me, this may be your first step-and-repeat, but with the way you sing, it won't be your last. Now come on, they're waiting for the birthday girl. Watch me and do what I do."

Mr. Versey gave me a reassuring smile, so I let him take my hand and guide me out of the SUV. When Hailey Joanne stepped out, the photographers forgot all about the mayor and started clamoring for her to "Look this way!" "Hailey Joanne, smile!" "Give us an over-the-shoulder!" "Over here, Hailey Joanne—you look beautiful!"

I made my way along the red carpet, staying about ten feet behind the birthday girl, and not one photographer noticed me. I was grateful. There was no way I could have handled all of the attention the way Hailey Joanne did.

In the lobby, Hailey Joanne made sure I got in since I had given my invitation to Izzy, and she was whisked away to a secret place to make her grand entrance. The theme of the party was Hollywood Glamour, and the party planner had gone crazy with decorations. Giant lights arced across the ceiling, and old-fashioned movie cameras and director's chairs were all around the ballroom. The dance floor was right out of the movies; it lit up as you stepped on it. There were posters from famous movies like *The Sound of Music* and *The Wizard of Oz*, but when I looked closely, all of the faces on the posters were Hailey Joanne's!

I was so completely dazzled by the décor that I almost forgot that the servers carrying trays of canapés were offering food that Dada had made. All of the people standing around smiling and munching on delicious delicacies were proof that my father was a master chef and caterer.

A server holding a tray of blue drinks in champagne flutes approached and lowered the tray to offer one. I thanked her, wondering how she could make it through the crowd balancing that tray with one hand. The drink was Dada's blueberry soda, and it was delicious.

As I sipped my drink, I spotted Izzy across the ballroom. She was wearing the really puffy balloon dress her mother created. It looked very high fashion—higher than anyone else in the room. I maneuvered myself around the edges of the dance floor, careful not to spill one drop of the dark-blue drink on my borrowed dress. I walked up behind Izzy and leaned close to her ear so I would be heard over the throbbing music the DJ was playing. "Hi!"

Izzy looked over her shoulder, smiled, said "Hi," and turned her attention back to the dance floor.

I tapped her on the shoulder. "Izzy. It's me!"

She stepped back, eyebrows raised, and looked me up and down. Slowly her eyebrows relaxed. "Mango! Is that you?" I nodded, and she screamed. "I can't believe it. I didn't recognize you. What happened to your face, your hair, your . . . everything?"

My stomach tightened; did I look that awful? "Hailey Joanne's glam squad gave me a makeover."

"They sure did."

"Is it bad?"

"No! Girl, you look incredible. . . . You just don't look like you. If I saw you on the street, I'd walk right by you. I'd be hating on you as I passed you by, because you look like a billion dollars, but I wouldn't know you at all."

"That's nice. . . . I guess."

Izzy whispered in my ear so she could be heard over the booming music. "How'd it go today?"

"Fine. Great. We had a lot of fun. For real."

"Good. So, where's the birthday girl?"

"She went off somewhere to get ready for her grand entrance."

Izzy grabbed my hand and pulled me forward. "Come on, let's dance!" I gulped my soda and placed the empty glass on a table before stepping onto the flashing lights of the dance floor.

After about twenty minutes of nonstop dancing, the music faded and all the lights went out. I was thinking there might be some sort of disastrous power outage when a booming voice over the speakers said, "Attention, please. Everyone welcome the birthday girl, Hailey Joanne Pinkey!" The giant spotlights lit up, swirling around the room before pointing up to the ceiling. There, seated on a swing high above the crowd, was Hailey Joanne!

Everyone hooted and applauded as the music kicked in and she was lowered slowly. I was so excited and overwhelmed, tears came to my eyes. Happy tears. I was happy for a girl who had treated me like we had been best friends all our lives, even though we'd only been hanging out for a little over a month. As I watched her descend to the dance floor, her smile brilliant, her dress sparkling, I wondered if underneath all that glitter, Hailey Joanne was just a lonely girl using all the things she had to make people like and admire her.

As she reached the floor, the crowd surged toward the guest of honor, but a squadron of burly guys wearing suits and dark glasses like the Secret Service held them back. I knew that after Hailey Joanne's parents made announcements and introduced celebrities and dignitaries, it would be time for TJ and the Halfrican Americans to perform and I'd be expected to be backstage, ready for our duet. I wondered what TJ would say when he saw me. Would he still be upset with me?

I was hoping that, after the party was over and Dada was officially a big success, I could go back to being myself around him. And what about Hailey Joanne? Would telling her the truth mess up our becoming friends? And could we remain friends even if we liked the same boy?

On my way to the stage, I stopped by the swinging doors to the kitchen. Having a father in the restaurant business, I knew enough to steer clear of those doors, because bustling waiters could burst out of them at any minute. Still, I wanted to congratulate Dada, so I carefully peeked inside the kitchen. There he was, wearing his chef whites and a tall column hat. He was so busy with all of the cooking staff and waiters buzzing around him that I decided not to interrupt. There would be plenty of time for celebrating him after the party.

I walked a few steps away from the door and bumped into—"Mom!"

She looked up at me. With my six-inch heels, I was taller than my mother for the first time. She said, "Mango Delight Fuller? What in the world?" She grabbed me by the hand and pulled me into the ladies' room just off the side of the backstage stairs.

"Ow! Mom, let go. You're hurting me."

She dropped my hand, and her fists went immediately to her hips. "What do you think you're doing, dressed and made up like that?"

"Like what? I look good."

"You look like a . . . I don't even want to say what you look like. Get over to the sink and wash that gunk off your face."

I couldn't believe she was reacting like this. Hailey Joanne, the glam squad, and Izzy all said I looked great. Why couldn't my own mother be happy for me and say something nice? She never had anything nice to say about women who wore makeup. That was not fair at all, so I said, "No, I can't wash it off. I have to perform in a few minutes, and . . . and I look good!"

"You may look good, but you don't look like my daughter or any twelve-year-old girl I would want you to know." She reached for my head, and I leaned away. "What did you do to your hair? You know you're not allowed to use chemicals in your hair, Mango."

"Mr. Horatio didn't use chemicals. It's all herbal stuff from Africa, brought over by slaves!"

Mom's eyes flashed with hot temper. "Are you kidding me? You just believed what some fool hairdresser told you? I ought to . . ." She closed her eyes and took a deep breath. "Mango, I thought you were smarter than that."

I pressed my fingertips to my eyes to prevent the teardrops from falling and ruining my makeup (a trick I learned watching heavily made-up rich housewives on reality TV shows). "I have to sing in a few minutes, Mom. May I go, please?"

Mom sighed. "Mango, I trusted that you would have better sense than to let people trick you into doing something that doesn't reflect who you really are." She flipped her hands into the air in a sign of surrender. "We need to have a long talk when you get home. Go on. Sing. Have a good show."

I walked past her out of the restroom. There was a line of girls waiting to get in. I suddenly felt ugly because my mother was ashamed of me. The weight of her disapproval felt like a thousand pounds of kettle bells hanging around my shoulders. But I didn't want to stumble or fall in front of her or all the people watching me, so I held my head high, arched my back, and walked toward the backstage stairs whispering over and over to myself, "I am Diana Ross. I *am* Diana Ross."

The backstage area was created by a series of black curtains. It was a very small space, but I needed to find a place to be alone, just for a few minutes so I could pull myself together. The Halfrican Americans, except for TJ, were standing in the wings waiting to go on. They all said hello to me, but I just waved and went on looking for a place to hide.

I hurried along a short corridor of curtain and turned into an area I thought would be empty, but there were two people there in the dark. Kissing.

The loud speakers announced, "Ladies and gentlemen, let's give a big round of applause and welcome the Halfrican Americans!"

The guy who was kissing the girl pulled away from her and parted the curtain. Light flooded in, and I saw TJ heading for the stage and Hailey Joanne holding the curtain open, watching him leave. I couldn't help myself, I screamed.

Hailey Joanne noticed me and said, "Mango? What are you doing back here?"

I ran. In six-inch heels, I ran away, down the stairs and through the crowd. I could hear Hailey Joanne calling after me, but I couldn't stop to face her or anyone. And I couldn't stop the tears falling from my eyes, smearing the masterpiece Sergio had painted on my face. I just kept running, and as I passed the kitchen doors, one of them flung open and I ran right into it. I was knocked backward and crashed into a waiter carrying a tray of blueberry soda. The glasses arced high into the air and, in what seemed like slow motion, blueberry soda rained down all over me, drenching my vintage Halston dress.

The Halfrican Americans were kicking off their first song, but none of the crowd near me paid any attention to the stage. Their eyes were glued to the freak on the floor surrounded by broken glass in a puddle of blueberry humiliation on the worst day of her entire life.

As if by magic, Mom suddenly appeared standing over me. She held out her hand, helped me off the floor, and led me out the back exit of the hotel and into a taxicab that took us home.

CHAPTER 18

Old Enough to Know

During the cab ride home, I sat as far away from Mom as I could. I curled into myself facing the window, clenching my jaw tight as a vise. I would not cry. I would have rather died than cry in the taxi with Mom.

Back in our apartment, while I peeled off the sticky Halston dress, Mom ran a hot bath for me. She put fragrant aromatherapy oils in the water and lit candles. All were meant to soothe me, but they didn't work. To stop myself from crying, I concentrated on hardening my heart to everything that had happened.

Yes, I saw Hailey Joanne kissing TJ. #IDONTCARE

Yes, I thought TJ liked me, but he likes her better. #IDONTCARE

Yes, I made a fool of myself in front of everyone. #IDONTCARE

If I could convince myself that I didn't care about anything, then nothing could bother me, right?

For the first time since maybe second grade, Mom stayed

in the bathroom and sat on a stool to bathe me. I didn't care. She removed the sticky, clip-on hairpieces and tossed them into the trash can. I didn't care. I closed dry eyes as she peeled my long, false eyelashes off. I didn't care. She smeared my face with Vaseline to wipe off the layers of makeup. I didn't care. Even soaking in the fragrant, steaming-hot bath water, I was a block of ice.

Mom lathered up a loofah sponge and began to wash my shoulders and back. She said, "You know, Mango, you can let go."

"Of what?"

"Your feelings, honey. You are like one big knot. Relax and release. You'll feel better if you cry."

"I'm not going to cry."

"Why not?"

For the first time since we left the hotel, I turned to look at Mom and narrowed my eyes. "*You* don't cry. I've never seen you cry. Aunt Zendaya said you didn't even cry when they told you that you would have to lose your leg."

Mom sat back on the stool, let the loofah fall into the water, and wiped her hands on her jeans. "That's not true."

"What's not true?"

"That I didn't cry. Your aunt doesn't know what she's talking about. You shouldn't listen to her."

"You never talk about it."

"I'll talk to you about it when you're ready. When you're old enough."

"I'm old enough now, Mom."

I noticed her hand trembling as she raised it to her forehead to wipe away beads of perspiration. She noticed it, too, because she grabbed it with her other hand, stood, and walked out of the bathroom.

I sat back in the tub, amazed that I had the nerve to bring up the subject Mom never talked about. I had rattled her. Maybe I'd hurt her. I felt a frog beginning to grow in my throat. I swallowed it.

#IDONTCARE

The water temperature had dropped to just below lukewarm when I finally got out of the tub, toweled off, put on my pajamas and robe, and walked out of the bathroom. Mom called to me from her bedroom. I didn't want to talk to her or anyone. I just wanted to get in bed and try to sleep forever. But she said, "Mango, please," and there was a tremor in her voice that I'd never heard before. I sighed and dragged myself to her room.

She was on the bed. A tray with two mugs of what smelled like peppermint tea sat on the night table, and her false leg was on the floor. She patted the bed next to her and said, "Come."

I crawled onto Dada's side of the bed, lifted my knees to my chest, and folded my arms tight around me. Mom lifted a mug of tea and held it out to me. I shook my head. She brought the mug to her mouth, blew on the tea, and sipped.

"You know my parents died when I was seventeen."

I nodded, looking toward the hallway, where I could see that I had left the bathroom light on. Normally, Mom would make me go back and turn it off right away, but this night was anything but normal.

"I had a full-ride scholarship to UCLA. A coach out there wanted to train me, because the university thought if I worked hard enough, I might be able to qualify for the Olympics." Mom kind of chuckled and shook her head. "I didn't know about that, but I thought my future was set. Then life hit me head-on like a freight train. My parents—two homebodies who never went anywhere—got all dressed up one night and went to a hole-in-the-wall social club in the Bronx to celebrate a coworker's birthday. They got trapped in a horrible fire. Newspapers said the owner of the club had blocked all the exits to stop people from sneaking in without paying. The one exit they could have escaped through was upstairs, and that's where the fire started. I mean, really, what kind of world . . . ?"

My shoulders began to soften. I uncrossed my arms and let my legs drop away from my chest. There was a picture of her mom and dad, the grandparents I'd never met, on Mom's night table. It was in a small, tarnished-silver frame and kind of clouded by the steam rising from the other mug of tea, but I could see they were smiling with their arms around each other. I realized I hadn't really looked at that photograph in years. I couldn't remember the last time I'd even considered them.

Mom was staring down into her mug of tea as if there were a code or a secret she was struggling to decipher at the bottom. I cleared my throat to get her attention, but it didn't work. Finally, I said, "Mom?"

"Huh? Oh, yeah. Well, needless to say, I didn't go to UCLA."

"Why not?"

"I couldn't go all the way to Los Angeles and leave Dora all by herself."

"You mean Aunt Zendaya?"

"She was Dora back then, before she became some kind of . . . I don't know what. A free-thinking, radical/liberal pacifist—or whatever she's calling herself nowadays."

"She's calling herself Zendaya," I said, reaching for Mom's mug of tea. She let me take it and picked up the one on the night table. She had sweetened the tea with just the right amount of honey. It felt good going down.

"Well, she was only fourteen back then. I was the older sister. I was responsible for her from the day she was born. Both my parents worked, and I was always left in charge of Dor—Zendaya. So I turned down the scholarship at UCLA and got a grant to do track at Brooklyn College and a part-time job. With the insurance money my parents left behind, we were okay, though I had to be careful with our budget."

"So, that's how you got to be the way you are."

"What are you trying to say?"

I giggled. "Good with money. Uh . . . frugal."

"Whatever." She smiled. We both sipped our tea, and she looked over at me. "You sure you're old enough to hear the rest?"

"I'm sure."

Mom cleared her throat. "A couple of years later, Zendaya was sixteen, and she had a little boyfriend who lived down the block. He called himself some kind of rapper or beatboxer or whatnot. I couldn't stand him, but I knew the harder I tried to keep her away from him, the more she'd want to be with him, so I gave them a long leash."

Mom took a deep breath, blew it out through her lips, and leaned back on the headboard. "There was some kind of all-day hiphop festival over on Staten Island, and, against my better judgment, I let her go with her boyfriend and their friends. She was supposed to be home by ten o'clock at night. When she didn't come back on time, I worried. When she didn't come back after midnight, I began to panic. I blamed myself for being too lenient. As the hours dragged on, I could hardly catch my breath. When she finally stepped in the door after four o'clock in the morning, I went ballistic."

I sat up straight and moved in closer to Mom. She balled her fists and squeezed them real tight and then released her fingers and shook them out.

"She claimed they had missed the last ferry and had to find a ride over the Verazzano Bridge back to Manhattan and then take a train to Brooklyn."

"Didn't you believe her?"

"Believe her? That didn't matter to me. She should have

got to a pay phone and called me! She put me through torture, Mango. She was like my child. We had just lost our parents two years before. I almost went out of my mind when she said she didn't call because she 'didn't want to wake me.' How could she imagine I would be asleep?"

Mom slammed her mug on the nightstand, and a bit of tea sloshed over the side. She covered her face with her hands, shook her head, and sighed deep. She reached behind her head and pulled off the band she used to put her dreads into a ponytail, shaking her hair loose. Her face had reddened and her eyes were like black marbles, growing harder and darker by the second. It was as though she was being pulled back twenty years, experiencing that night all over again. No wonder she never wanted to talk about it. But I had to know.

"What happened next, Mom?"

She rubbed her temples as she went on. "I don't know what came over me, but I put my hands on my sister. I hit her. My parents had never laid a hand on either one of us, but I just snapped and couldn't stop myself. Afterward I tried to apologize, but Zendaya pushed me away. She screamed that she hated me, that I wasn't her mother, and that she wished *I* were dead instead of our parents. At that moment, so did I."

Mom's hand found one of her dreads, and she began to twist it around and around in her fingers. "I grabbed my keys and got into my half-broken-down car and took off. I wasn't sure where I was going at first, but I found myself driving toward Brooklyn College. The streets were pretty empty at that time of morning. It was dark, and I was in fifth gear—pedal to the metal. I was rushing to get to the track; that was the only place where I could lose myself. Lose the pain I was feeling. The guilt. The regret. All of it. I just wanted it gone.

"As I approached the college, I wasn't thinking, I wasn't . . . I don't know. I guess I wasn't seeing where I was going. I ran a red light. Two cars came at me from opposite directions, and . . ." She winced at the memory, breathed deep, and shuddered.

"When I woke up, there were sirens. Lights were flashing all around. Firemen were trying to get the car open with the Jaws of Life. Helicopters—I heard the sound of their blades whirring overhead. Then I guess I passed out again. Later I learned that I had made the morning news. That's how Zendaya found out—when she saw what was left of the car on TV."

I moved in close to Mom and touched her shoulder. "I'm sorry."

She put her arm around me and pulled me close. "Zendaya was the first person I saw when I came to in the hospital. She was a wreck, sobbing and saying how sorry she was. Then the doctor told me they would have to amputate my leg. And you were right: I didn't cry. In that moment, I *couldn't* cry.

"See, if I cried, my baby sister—the person I was responsible for—she would blame herself for what happened for the rest of her life. So I held my tears back with everything I had in me. This was *my* fault. And after what I had done, I deserved what I got. So I didn't cry. At least, not when anyone could see."

I sat up and looked at Mom. Tears were falling from her eyes. I held her face in my hands and did my best to kiss them away.

#IDIDCARE

CHAPTER 19

Truth Hurts

The stained vintage Halston dress taunted me from where it hung on a hanger across the room on the door to my closet. We were going to have to send the dress to a specialty cleaner before we returned it to Tessica. A part of me wanted to hide it, but the bigger part of me demanded I let it hang there in full view to remind me of the worst night of my life. Even though what happened to me at the party was nothing compared to the worst night of my mom's life, it still hurt.

Maybe Mom was right and I wasn't ready to hear the whole story yet. Feelings I had for what happened to her and feelings about what happened to me mixed and melded until I couldn't separate them. All I wanted to do was escape into sleep. That was the only place where I could get away from everything that had happened at the party and everything I had learned.

—

On Monday morning, I couldn't face going back to school. When Mom came to wake me, I croaked that my throat hurt, and even though I knew she didn't believe me, she let me be. Maybe it was because this was her first day back at work. She would have to stand for hours on a false leg that didn't fit perfectly anymore. She wasn't going back to work because she loved her job—being a retail manager was not her dream. She did it because she had to.

Later that morning I sat up in bed, rubbed my eyes, and wondered why she wasn't at my bedside, lecturing me on finding my strength and following her example of doing what was expected of you no matter what. Maybe she was tired of me. I was certainly tired of myself.

Around eleven o'clock, Dada burst into my room, handed me a smoothie, and said, "Get dressed. We're going for a run in the park."

I hadn't run since the day I'd tripped over the tree root and skinned my knee. Back when I was in GOT training, sometimes I would run through the park with Dada on weekends. I'd listen to music as I ran, but Dada never would. "Shut out the world with headphones? No way, *mon*. The sounds of the city, the cars honking, buses wheezing, birds chirping—that is music enough for me."

The banana-strawberry-kale smoothie was incredible. And although I kind of resented being ordered to get up, I knew I'd have to leave my room sooner or later.

We set out for the park. At the corner, I realized I'd forgotten my MP3 player and headphones. "I have to go back. I can't run without music."

"Yes, you can."

"I know I *can*, Dada, but I don't want to."

He put a hand on my shoulder. "Mango, you've never forgotten your music before, have you?"

"No."

"Well, think about it. Maybe you left it behind for a reason. Maybe you need to experience your run differently today. Maybe—just maybe—you need this time to think about things and see yourself without distractions."

My Dada could be so . . . Zen sometimes. His almond eyes regarded me with such love, I had to give in. I shrugged. "Okay. But I have a feeling this is going to be like eating cornflakes without milk." Dada laughed, and we walked to the park.

It was a perfect day for running. A steady breeze put a chill in the air that complemented the warmth of the sun. The trees were showing off their blossoms, fluffy and colorful. I had barely noticed the wonders of summer, being so wrapped up in rehearsing the play, fake-friending Hailey Joanne, and hiding my feelings for TJ. But even though I was busy with all my personal drama, the world didn't stop. Flowers bloomed, bees pollinated, and baby birds hatched. Regardless of how down I felt, the world kept moving onward and upward. The realization made me smile. Nothing could stop what was meant to be. The only thing standing in my way was me.

When we had finished running through the park, I was exhausted but feeling good. The dark fog that had overtaken me had lifted, burned off by the sun and blown away on the breeze. As we crossed Martin Luther King Boulevard, Dada held his hand out the way he used to do when I was small. My hand lifted to his automatically. My eyes began to water, and I had to bite my bottom lip to stop it from trembling.

Dada squeezed my hand. "Are you all right?"

I nodded. "Yes. I'm fine. I'm great."

"Then why are you about to cry?"

"Because you reached for my hand, and I love you so much. You, Mom, Jasper . . . you didn't turn your back on me when I messed things up. You loved me anyway."

"Of course, Mango. Family loves you whether you're on top of the hill or deep in the valley. Unconditional. That is the only kind of love that counts."

As we approached a bodega, Dada dug some change out of his sweatpants and bought a newspaper. "When we get home, we can go through this newspaper together, read about all the troubles in the world, and compare them to yours. How do you think you'll measure up?"

I laughed. "Not at all?"

"That's right. Not a blip on the radar. That's a reason to be grateful for life and all the things it brings to you, positive and negative."

"I'm not grateful for the negative."

"Why not? Without the bad, you wouldn't appreciate the good. You'd probably be bored to death. Life without conflict, challenges, or pain is dull, like food with no spice—bland, unsatisfying, *a waste for de taste, mon*." He laughed at his silly rhyme, and it was contagious.

By the time we reached home, I had decided that I'd had enough of hiding in my room. I told Dada that I wanted to go to school. I could get there in time for rehearsal. This afternoon we were scheduled to do our first run-through of the entire play, from beginning to end with the full orchestra. It was my responsibility to do what was right and not let the cast, Bob, and Mr. Ramsey down.

I arrived at school just before rehearsal started. My old friend the mango pit was growing in my belly, because I didn't know how I would react when I saw TJ. What would I tell him about not showing up to sing our duet at the party? Before I could reach the auditorium, Izzy saw me in the hall and pulled me into the girls' bathroom.

"What happened to you on Saturday? I thought you were going to sing with TJ! I called on Sunday, but your mom said you were sleeping. Somebody said you got sick and had to be taken away in an ambulance. What happened? Was it food poisoning? That's what some people were saying, but the food was amazing!"

"It wasn't food poisoning."

"Then what was it?"

"Never mind. I'm fine now."

"Are you sure? Why weren't you in school today?"

"I . . . uh . . . Mental-health day, you know . . ."

"Okay. Helen Keller could see you don't want to talk about it, and I'm not the kind of friend who pries into people's business."

Izzy shrugged. I could tell she was a little peeved that I wouldn't confide in her, but I just couldn't. Not right then. I still had to face TJ and, eventually, Hailey Joanne. I didn't know how I would handle any of that, and I didn't want to have to talk about it before coming face-to-face with them. I gave Izzy a hug and whispered in her ear, "Thanks for understanding."

The entire cast and crew were assembled in the auditorium. Bob and Mr. Ramsey sat on the lip of the stage and explained that the first run-through of any show never goes smoothly, and we might not make it through the entire play, but that was to be expected. This is when we would run into all the kinks in cues and blocking and work them out one by one. "So don't be discouraged or hard on yourselves or each other. This will be a slog, so let's all do our best, but be prepared for the worst. Okay, places for act one, scene one!"

As I hurried stage right, where I would make my first

entrance, TJ ran up behind me. "Hey, um, are you okay? What happened Saturday night?"

I stopped and turned to him but couldn't lift my eyes from the floor. "Oh, it was nothing. Something I ate, maybe. Can we talk about this later?"

"Sure." He put a hand on my shoulder. "I was worried about you is all, but if you're okay, I'm cool." He took off for stage left, where he would make his first entrance. I wondered if I had just thrown Dada under the bus by saying it was something I ate. Why did I lie? Of course, I couldn't tell TJ the real reason I ran away, not before I cleared the air with Hailey Joanne.

While I waited for my entrance cue, I took some deep breaths and told myself to calm down and concentrate on the play. I was Juliet, a pop superstar, confident and talented and on the way to the greatest adventure of her life. I realized for the first time that it was nice to have a character to escape into, to hide behind, when things in your real life got tough.

Bob and Mr. Ramsey ended up being right: there were hundreds of kinks to work out, and we had barely made it through the first act before rehearsal was over and we were released. I sort of hung out in a dressing room until almost everyone was gone. I was avoiding walking home with Izzy and the questions she would bring up. And, of course, I didn't want to see TJ when we were offstage and out of character.

When I thought the coast was clear, I slipped out the

backstage exit and walked the long way around the building. Wind pushed heavy, dark clouds slowly across the sky, like whales. I could smell rain in the air and knew I'd have to hurry home if I didn't want to get drenched.

To my surprise and horror, a familiar black SUV with tinted windows was idling at the curb. The driver's door opened, and Mr. Versey stepped out. "Good evening, Miss Mango. Miss Hailey Joanne would like to offer you a ride home." He opened the back door, and there was Hailey Joanne on her cell phone, waving at me to get in.

I wanted to run. Maybe I should have, but I knew I couldn't avoid this moment for the rest of my life, so I sighed and climbed into the cave-like darkness of the SUV.

As Mr. Versey pulled away from the school and merged into heavy traffic, rain began to fall hard. Hailey Joanne finished an angry conversation that I could tell was with her mother. She clicked off her phone and then reached over and touched my hand tenderly. "Are you all right? What happened to you at the party? I saw you scream and run off. I tried to chase you, but there was no way I could keep up with the six-inch heels I was wearing. What happened? Why did you scream like that?"

I slid my hand from beneath hers and turned to look out the rain-splattered window. What should I say? This was the moment of truth, so to speak. If I made up some excuse, I would have to carry it around and pretend it was the truth forever. That's a huge burden. Also, I would just be flat-out lying. I had already lied to TJ. It was a little lie, but it was a lie just the same. If I turned to Hailey Joanne and lied now, that would be it—Mango Delight Fuller would be a liar for sure. I might get away with it because no one had any idea what really made me freak out, but *I* would know the truth, and every time I looked at myself in the mirror, I would be looking into the face of a liar. I couldn't do that to myself. I had to tell the truth, for me.

Besides, I had grown to like Hailey Joanne for real, and I wanted us to be friends with nothing fake between us. I was faking when Brook first got her phone, pretending I was so happy for her when I really felt envious and afraid. If I'd been honest from the beginning, things might have turned out differently. Maybe if I was completely honest now, there could be a way for us to truly be friends.

It was so hard, but I turned to face Hailey Joanne and said, "I got upset and screamed backstage . . . because I saw you and TJ kissing."

Hailey Joanne's eyebrows shot up in surprise. "Why would that make you scream? You know I like him. I've been telling you about it for weeks. I don't understand how that would upset you."

I felt as though I was on the edge of a cliff. Hundreds of feet below me were jagged rocks with waves crashing into them. I couldn't breathe for a minute, thinking that I had no choice but to tell the truth no matter what happened. Would I splash into the water, or land on the rocks? Either way, I had to jump. "I . . . like him, too." There. I had jumped, and I was falling.

Hailey Joanne sat back and looked at me with her head cocked to the side. "Why didn't you tell me? Why did you just listen to me go on and on about him? You even encouraged me."

"I didn't want to upset you." I was falling faster and tumbling, my stomach lurching into my throat, but there was no way to stop now. "I was afraid that if you were mad at me, you'd fire my father and find another caterer for your party."

Hailey Joanne's lips tightened as she looked down at her freshly manicured fingernails, and then she turned away from me, looking out the window. The *whomp whomp* of the windshield wipers counted off the long seconds that poured between us like sand filling an hourglass. Car horns were blaring outside the window as we inched forward in traffic. Finally, I said, "I'm sorry."

Hailey Joanne whirled on me. There were tears in her eyes. "Don't be. It's not the first time I've been used, and I'm sure it won't be the last."

She was right; I had used her. Even though I thought I had a good reason, was it really an excuse to treat her so badly? How could she ever know who her real friends were when people like me took advantage of her? I felt ugly inside, charred and shriveled like a cigarette smoker's lung. I said, "I'm really sorry, Hailey—"

She lifted her hand and cut me off. "I can't hear a word

you're saying." She shouted, "Versey, stop the car! Mango is getting out here."

Mr. Versey said, "But, Miss Hailey Joanne, it's raining mighty hard."

Hailey Joanne snapped, "Did I ask you for a weather report? Open the door and put her out!"

Mr. Versey made eye contact with me in the rearview mirror for a brief instant and kept on moving forward, inch by inch, in the bumper-to-bumper traffic.

Hailey Joanne screamed, "Versey! Do as I say, or . . ."

"Or what, Miss Hailey Joanne?"

"I swear I'll fire you!"

"You go on and do what you have to do, Miss Hailey Joanne, but I'll put *you* out in the street before I let this poor child walk all the way home in this storm."

Hailey Joanne threw a tantrum. You know, the kind little kids have when they scream and bang their fists and kick their feet. I moved as close to the door as I could get to keep out of the way of her flailing limbs.

Finally, when she had worn herself out, she dropped her head onto her knees and sobbed until she fell asleep. It was unbelievable, but by the time Mr. Versey pulled up to my building, she was actually snoring.

Mr. Versey hurried around to the passenger door and opened a huge black umbrella. I looked at Hailey Joanne, and, even though I didn't think she would hear me over her snoring, I said, "I'm really, truly sorry."

Mr. Versey escorted me to the entrance of my building. He said, "You did good. She needed to hear the truth."

I nodded, thanked him for the ride, and went inside.

Riding up on the elevator, I tried hard not to cry. I made myself think about how Dada loved my tomato, arugula, and grilled cheese sandwich. I used cheddar and Swiss cheese— two slices of each with a few leaves of arugula between them. I sliced the tomato very thin and buttered the inside of both pieces of the bread. I spread mayonnaise on the outside (that makes the bread golden brown and gives it the perfect crunch). I put the sandwich in a hot pan and use another pan to smash it down really good and cook both sides until the cheese was melted to the point that it started to squish out from the bread. Delicious! By the time I reached my floor, I had avoided crying, but I still couldn't get the image of Hailey Joanne's tantrum out of my head, and the fact that I had caused it made me feel the need to start thinking of another recipe quick.

CHAPTER 20

The Big News

When I opened the door to our apartment, the earthy aroma of brown stewed fish embraced me. Bob Marley's "Three Little Birds" was blaring from the speakers and there was laughter coming from the kitchen. There, I found Mom and Dada dancing and singing while Jasper watched from his high chair, clapping and bopping to the song.

Jasper spied me first and cried out, "Maga! Maga!" As Mom and Dada turned to look at me, the smiles on their faces told me something wonderful had happened. I lifted Jasper out of his high chair, sat with him on my lap, and said, imitating Dada's accent, *"What a gwan?"*

Dada turned the music down, cleared his throat, and said, "Thanks to you, my sweet Mango Delight, I received a call from the mayor's wife this afternoon. They are hiring me to cater their daughter's wedding and maybe more events for City Hall!" Dada leapt up into the air, clapping and laughing. Mom was laughing, too. I was happy and did my best to eke out a smile, but it wasn't convincing at all.

Mom said, "Mango, what's the matter with you?"

I didn't want to tell another lie, but the truth was just too heavy for a time that called for celebration, and I didn't want to ruin it. But if I was going to be an honest person, I couldn't turn back now just because it was convenient. So I said, "I really don't want to talk about this now, but I'll just say . . . I hurt someone's feelings today. I never wanted to, but I did, and I don't feel good about it."

Mom said, "Who?"

"Mom, please, this is something I need to deal with on my own. Please. May I be excused?"

Dada knelt in front of me. "I understand, sweetie. Why don't you go lie down? You want me to bring your dinner to your room?"

I handed Jasper to him and said, "No, I'm not hungry."

Mom said, "But you love brown stewed fish."

Dada nodded with a crinkle of concern around his eyes. "You usually gobble it up like a harbor shark." He put his hand to my head. "You have a fever?"

"No. No, I'm fine. I just have a lot on my mind." I walked past them, went into my room, and crawled under the covers, still in my clothes. That's where I stayed until the next morning.

School dragged by for the rest of the week, except for when we were in rehearsal. I was so anxious to escape inside my character that I couldn't wait to hit the stage. Bob and Mr.

Ramsey said my performances were getting stronger and my voice sounded better than ever. Bob said, "Whatever you're doing, keep on doing it! It's working!"

Right. Keep on being miserable in real life. If that's the secret to being good on stage, I think I'd better choose another career.

When TJ and I were onstage together and in character, we really connected as Juliet and Romeo. Offstage, it was still awkward but not in a bad way. Boss Chloe told me her "little birds" saw him in the mall coming out of the multiplex theater with Hailey Joanne, so they were probably boyfriend and girlfriend now. That hurt a little at first, but I did my best to get over it. We were boyfriend and girlfriend onstage, and that's what I'd have to settle for since I messed up any other chance of us being in a relationship.

I did my best to avoid Hailey Joanne, so our paths didn't cross at all—mostly because all the cast members were excused from eating lunch in the cafeteria until the show ended its one-weekend run. We spent our lunch period in the auditorium, eating together, running lines, rehearsing music, getting fitted for costumes, and testing makeup. I was now a full-fledged Dramanerd, and I enjoyed being with my cast mates. We all spoke the same language and shared the same silly jokes that no one would get if they weren't a part of our stage family. I was relieved and pretty happy—except, surprisingly, a part of me missed Hailey Joanne.

The week of tech rehearsals flew by. We ran through the play in costumes and would have to stop and hold our places, sometimes for fifteen or twenty minutes, while the big lights that hung above the stage were adjusted, focused, and gelled. We were like race horses at the gate ready to run; we were anxious to perform for an audience but had to give the crew time to perfect their part of the show.

There was one long hold when the crew was lighting the recording booth scene where Romeo and Juliet fall in love. We had nothing to do but hold our places and wait while the lighting guys moved the scaffold in and scrambled above us, focusing the special "love lights." I could sense that TJ wasn't nervous around me anymore, because he didn't blurt out any obscure factoids. He simply waited. I simply waited. We were like two people in an elevator just waiting to get off on different floors.

Finally, I said, "How's Hailey Joanne?"

"She's fine. I guess. Why?"

"No reason. I thought you two were dating now."

"Why would you think that?" There was a bit of *odditude* in his voice, like he was surprised at what I said and irritated by it, so I thought I'd better back off.

"No reason. Never mind. Forget it."

He went on. "You're the one who's got the wrong impression for some reason."

"Someone saw you coming out of the movie theater with her."

"Uh . . . I don't know what your little spies have told you, but I didn't go to the movies with her. We ran into each other on the way out of separate theaters and spoke for a minute, but that was it. So tell your spies to get their stories straight, okay?"

I was fuming. How dare he talk to me like I was some little kid or something? I said, "I saw you kissing her backstage at her birthday party with my own eyes. I didn't need spies for that, TJ."

I was about to walk offstage when Bob called from the audience, "All right, we're ready to move on. Take it from the top of 'Duet Forever.'"

The orchestra started playing. I turned away from TJ. He whispered, "You're supposed to be looking at me."

I didn't turn to look at him. "I'd rather eat a bowl of rabbit turds."

TJ began to sing. When my part came, I sang it without looking at him; I just couldn't. As the song progressed, I slowly got back into character and turned to look at him just before we had to kiss. I looked up into his kiwi-green eyes. They were moist, on the verge of tears. I reached for his hands, and he took mine. We moved together slowly and kissed as the lights faded to a blackout.

There were whoops, shouts, and applause from the audience. Bob called for house lights and rushed up onto the stage. He called the cast onstage from the wings, "Did you guys see that? Did you?" He turned to me. "Mango, that was an amazing choice, to turn away from him until the end of the song. It was so powerful. And, TJ, the longing in your eyes was . . . oh, it was magnetic!"

Bob turned to the rest of the cast. "You see, kids, this is what real actors do. They keep exploring and taking risks, being in the moment and staying in character. We've been rehearsing for six weeks, and we all think we've got the show down pat, but I want you to understand that there is still time for discoveries and surprises. That's what makes the theater vital and unique. Every performance is different, night after night." He turned back to TJ and me. "Keep up the great work. Keep exploring. You're amazing, both of you." He clapped us both on the shoulders and called for a five-minute break.

As the cast scattered, TJ and I just stood there for a moment and looked at each other, both of us about to burst out laughing. We ran backstage, and, as soon as almost everyone had cleared out, we let go and had a long laugh. TJ said, "How did that happen?"

"I don't know. Maybe we should try to get mad at each other before every show?"

"I'm not mad at you, Mango. I thought you were mad at me for the longest time. I mean, at one point we were . . . friends. But after that time in my garage—"

"I'm sorry. I acted like that because . . ."

"I know. Hailey Joanne told me what was going on when I

saw her in the lobby at the movies. She's really hurt. She felt like you were using her."

"I was. I guess. I mean, I came to really like her, but yeah, I didn't mean to hurt her feelings."

"You pretended to be her friend because of your dad. I understand. Hey, listen, sometimes we all do stupid things for the right reasons. That's just life. It's not too late to make up for it. I mean, you're both still breathing, right?"

"Right." He was being so cool. How could anyone not like him? I didn't know what to say, so I didn't say anything.

We just stood there looking away from each other, neither one of us wanting to leave.

"Just so you know, sometimes I do stupid things for the right reasons, too," he said.

"Like what?"

"That night, at the birthday party." He took a deep breath and let it out slowly. "Yeah, I did kiss Hailey Joanne. I knew she kind of liked me. I mean, that's why she gave my band the gig, right? So when she caught me backstage and asked for a birthday kiss . . . I couldn't refuse. I didn't want to make her mad. . . ."

"Or hurt her feelings?"

"Yeah, that too." He shook his head, shrugged his shoulders, took a deep breath, and blew it out through his lips. "That day at the mall, we had a long talk. I told her I thought she was cool and beautiful, but I liked someone else, so. . . ."

Boss Chloe yelled, "We're back. Places from where we left off. Let's go, people!"

I turned away from TJ and rushed back onto the stage. The lights went out, and the orchestra started playing the music that transitioned to the next scene. As scenery moved and I headed to my glow-in-the-dark tape mark, TJ held onto my arm and whispered, "It's you. I told her that you're the one I like."

The next scene was in Juliet's bedroom with Izzy as my agent. TJ's last words had left me so stunned that I floated through the rest of the play as if I were an airplane on autopilot.

At the end of rehearsal, Izzy cornered me in the girls' dressing room. "What's going on with you? Where was your mind today?"

"Was I that bad?"

"No, you were good, but . . ." She circled her index finger around her temple, making a cuckoo sign. "I don't know, you were just . . . out there."

"You think everyone could tell?"

"Of course not—they don't have a sick sense like me."

I giggled and led Izzy toward a dark corner just outside the dressing room. "TJ just told me. . . ."

"What? What?"

"He told me that he told Hailey Joanne that he liked me."

Izzy gasped, "Like? Or *like* like?"

"*Like* like!"

Izzy squealed out loud, and I covered her mouth. Braces Chloe stopped on her way to the dressing room and peered into the dark corner, but I don't think she saw us.

I uncovered Izzy's mouth. "This is between me and you. No one else. Promise?"

Izzy hugged me. "Cross my heart. I wouldn't do anything to mess this up for you!"

As we headed for the dressing room, I wasn't worried that Izzy would spread the news all over the school. I was sure I could trust her. I was sure we were that close.

Since rehearsals were running late this week, Dada showed up to drive me home. I saw TJ on the way out. We smiled and waved to each other. When I was seated in the car, I didn't mean to, but I shivered and let out a squeal. Dada smiled at me. "Good rehearsal?"

I beamed. "Yes. The best ever."

I looked out of the car window. It was dark, and I could see my reflection in the glass. I looked happy. TJ liked me, and I liked him—and not just because he liked me. I *really* liked him. That made me wonder about Hailey Joanne. She liked TJ, too, and he rejected her. I'm sure he did it in the nicest way possible, but it must have hurt. After all, two people she liked had used her.

The helium in the balloon of happiness I was floating on began to seep through a pinprick of guilt until, by the time we got home, my happiness was completely deflated. I couldn't just ignore what I had done to Hailey Joanne. I would have to face her, tell her how really sorry I was and confess how much I really had grown to like her. Maybe she'd forgive me, or maybe she wouldn't, but I had to do my part to make amends.

But when? How?

CHAPTER 21

The Big Gesture

The next few days leading up to opening night flew by. Run-throughs and dress rehearsals were going well, and so was my friendship with TJ. I liked him as much as he liked me, but I was only twelve—too young to have a boyfriend according to my mom. And Dada insisted I couldn't date until I was thirty years old. I know he was joking about the age, but I wasn't in a hurry. Right now, TJ and I were great friends. We had our lunches together in the auditorium, we talked and laughed a lot, and everyday he had a new factoid to share with me. "Did you know earthworms have five hearts?"

I began to look up obscure facts to share with him. One day when I had found a good one, I said, "Did you know a lobster's teeth are in its stomach?"

His eyebrows shot up. "Seriously? You want to go head-to-head on a factoid challenge with me?"

I said, "Yeah, buddy, you're on."

The obscure factoid competition had begun. Pretty soon the rest of the cast caught on, and we were all popping off odd facts at each other in rehearsals and even when we crossed paths in the school halls. . . .

"Did you know a male ostrich can roar like a lion?"

"Hot dogs can last more than twenty years in landfills!"

"Gorillas burp when they're happy."

"Cat urine glows under blacklights!"

Yes, our factoids grew grosser and grosser, but it was a fun game that bonded the entire cast and crew—especially TJ and me. One afternoon at lunch, I noticed that TJ and I were sitting together while the rest of the Dramanerds were hanging out having their lunch on the other side of the stage. It made me feel strange, like they didn't want to be around us. On the walk home from school, I asked Izzy about it.

"Don't worry about it, Mango, everyone is just giving you two space."

"What? Why? Do they know we like each other?"

"Of course they do!"

"How?"

Izzy smiled and sighed. "The way you two always eat lunch, giggle, and whisper your private jokes together. Everybody thinks it's real cute—well . . . almost everybody."

I looked at her. "Are you talking about who I think you're talking about?"

"I'm not saying any names, but her initials are Hailey Joanne Pinkey."

I couldn't laugh at Izzy's joke. "I feel horrible about deceiving her the way I did."

"I'm not the one you should be confessing to."

"I've tried to talk to her, but she won't answer my phone calls or even stop to speak to me in the halls."

"Then you have to find a big gesture."

"Come again?"

"A big gesture. Tía Maria Magdelena always said before she died in the car crash on the way to pay her bookie, '*Las acciones grande y más que las palabras*,' and she was right."

"Right about what? Translation, *por favor*?"

"It means 'big actions speak louder than words.' You've got to *do* something to show Hailey Joanne that you're sorry."

I thought about it for a moment and said, "Should I write her a letter?"

"Remember when you wrote a letter to Brooklyn? Remember how well that worked?"

Yes, I'd never forget how rejected and humiliated that made me feel. "So, what should I do?"

"Something big. Something public that lets Hailey Joanne and everyone know that you're sorry and you really care. And it has to be public; that way you're vulnerable and if she rejects you, you'll be humiliated. Like the people who propose marriage on the jumbotron at football games with the whole stadium watching. They risk getting rejected. See, you gotta put yourself on the line like that to make it count."

We arrived at Izzy's house, and she turned up the

walkway. I called after her, "Hey, aren't you going to help me figure out a big gesture?"

"Uh-uh. You've got to come up with that yourself. It's the price you pay to show you're really sorry. See ya!"

She went into her house, and I continued on home, trying to think of a gesture big enough to patch things up with Hailey Joanne and maybe—just maybe—help us be friends for real this time.

For the next few days, I tried to run into Hailey Joanne on purpose. The first time I saw her, Izzy and I were on our way to the auditorium, I called out, "Hailey Joanne! Hi!" She just nodded and kept on walking. Izzy shook her head. "Not big enough."

The day before the show, I got what I thought was a great idea. I rushed over to Hailey Joanne and held out an envelope to her. "This is for you. Two tickets to *Yo, Romeo!*'s opening night."

She stepped back as if I were handing her a bag of dog poop. "I already have tickets." As she walked off, I could hear Izzy in my ear. "Not big enough."

Finally, it was opening night. Excitement was so high backstage. Everyone was running around, getting into costumes and makeup, making sure their props were where they needed to be. I felt like a jet plane just waiting for the signal from the tower that would let me streak down the runway and take off. This was my first show. I had fallen into it by accident because of a trick that was supposed to humiliate me, but now my time was here. It was time to see if I really had what it takes to be onstage.

As I stood in the wings waiting for the orchestra to begin the overture and the show to start, my stomach was doing flip-flops like never before. I began panting, unable to catch my breath. Beads of sweat broke out on my forehead. Just then, someone tapped me on the shoulder. I turned to TJ, who should have been on the other side of the stage for his entrance. He smiled at me and said, "Did you know it's been proven that human boogers taste just like scrambled eggs."

I said "Ew!" and we both burst out laughing. He gave me a peck on the cheek, said, "Break a leg, rookie," and took off. Suddenly, all my nervousness and panic were gone. I was ready. This was going to be fun, because I was doing it with my friends.

The show went by at lightning speed. It was as though we were on a carousel going crazy fast. The more the audience reacted, the faster the carousel spun around and around. They applauded the songs, laughed at the funny parts, and got really quiet when Izzy, as my agent, announced that Romeo and Juliet's plane had disappeared in the Bermuda Triangle. And then the audience's spirits lifted again when we sang the rocking closing number as ghosts whose talent would live on through the ages. When the curtains closed, the cheers and applause from the audience were tremendous.

The curtains reopened, and it was time to take our bows. TJ and I waited backstage as the chorus walked onstage to applause, followed by the supporting cast. When Izzy stepped out, the applause and cheers ramped up. She deserved the boost, because she was fantastic. When it was time for TJ and me to step out onstage, he took my hand and we ran out to center stage together. The screaming and clapping was so loud, I thought the roof would lift off the auditorium.

As we had rehearsed, TJ stepped forward and bowed. Then it was my turn. This made me even more nervous than I was at the start of the show. As I stepped forward, I let myself look into the audience for the first time and immediately spotted Mom and Dada. They were both on their feet; Dada was cheering and had his arms around Mom, who was clapping and crying. Seriously, her face was shining with tears. I was stunned for an instant. Then I realized she was crying happy tears. I could tell, because she was smiling at the same time.

As I stood up from my bow, TJ stepped toward me with a huge bouquet of red roses that Bob and Mr. Ramsey had handed him from backstage. I accepted the roses, and the entire cast burst into applause for me. I was overwhelmed. I looked at all of them, smiling at me. It was as though I was the center of the universe, and I felt so grateful.

I turned and looked back out at the audience. That's when I saw her. Hailey Joanne was in her seat, applauding. She had actually come to the show, and she'd liked it. I didn't really think about what I did next—it just happened, because it was from the heart.

I walked down the stairs at the side of the stage and into the audience. The applause petered out. Everyone was watching, wondering where I was going and what I was going to do, but I didn't worry about it. I just followed my heart—right to Hailey Joanne's seat. I held out the bouquet of roses to her.

She could have pushed the roses away, or taken them and thrown them on the floor, but she did neither of those things. Hailey Joanne smiled at me and accepted the roses. I held out my arms, and we embraced. I whispered in her ear, "I am so sorry, Hailey Joanne. Can you ever forgive me?"

My eyes filled with tears when she whispered, "Yes. I forgive you."

As I made my way back to the stage, the audience resumed applauding. I took my place amongst the cast. We did a group bow, and the curtain closed. TJ gave me a big hug, and we headed off to our dressing rooms.

I was in front of the mirror wiping my makeup off when Izzy came up behind me and spoke to my reflection. "Now that's what I call a big gesture, girl!" She patted me on the back and walked off to take selfies with other cast members.

I looked at my reflection and smiled. If I had to go through all of what I went through to get to this moment again, I believed I would. I truly would, because everything that happened that led me to this place—all the tears, worry, laughs, and drama—everything was worth it.

CHAPTER 22

What Had Happened Was . . .

It turns out I didn't have to wait until I was fourteen years old to get a phone after all—Dada and Mom bought me one as an opening-night gift. The first person I texted was Hailey Joanne. We've been talking ever since. We're not besties. Not yet. But we're friends. And I've realized that maybe I don't need just *one* bestie anymore. TJ, Hailey Joanne, Izzy, the Chloes, and the rest of the cast—we all keep in touch and hang out and do things together, like seeing movies or just meeting up for lunch or hanging out in Izzy's basement listening to music.

Having a group of friends feels right for me now.

One Saturday long after the musical ended, Hailey Joanne had Mr. Versey pick me up and drive us out to the country club the Pinkeys belong to. It has an amazing running path around the golf course and through a wooded area that makes me feel like I'm in a fairy tale. Izzy was invited, too,

217

but she had no interest in spending the day running, and Hailey Joanne and I understood.

After a five-mile jog where Hailey Joanne and I kept the pace up by pushing and daring each other, we were completely winded. We plopped down on a cushion of pine needles by a pond where we could see turtles' heads popping up out of the water.

Hailey Joanne panted, "You know, you're really getting good. I have to work hard to keep up with you."

I laughed. "I'm the one who has to work to keep up with you!"

Hailey Joanne reached for her feet, beginning to stretch. "I'm serious. Next year, we're going to be the queens of GOT. No one will be able to keep up with us."

That was funny; I hadn't thought about going back to GOT next year. I kept up my running because I enjoyed it, but mostly because Mr. Ramsey told me it was a great way to increase my lung capacity and breath control for singing.

I started stretching and turned to Hailey Joanne. "You know, I don't think I'm going back to GOT."

"Why not? You won't be suspended anymore."

"I know—and don't get me wrong, I love running—but now I think I love singing and performing even more."

Hailey Joanne put a hand to her forehead and pretended to swoon. "Oh, well, now that you are a star, *dahh*ling!"

I laughed. "I'm not. But there *is* a drama club that meets after school to work on scenes and acting technique. I want to join that club. I want to study and really get good at it. And maybe when the spring musical comes around, I can audition without getting tricked into it and earn a part in the next show."

"You'll get a part, and you'll be great. But you have to promise me one thing."

"What?"

"That you'll keep running with me from time to time. You're a better motivator than Apps For Laps."

We giggled. I said, "I promise. Whenever you want a hard run, I'll be there."

"Crisp!" She leapt up. "How about now?" Hailey Joanne ran off. "Last one back to the clubhouse is a wet cheeseburger!"

I jumped up and powered after her. Pretty soon, with a little Beyoncé singing in my head, I was caught up and matching my friend stride for stride.

Acknowledgments

Every project I've created began as a misty image that led to a journey through the unknown. Along the way, like Dorothy in *The Wizard of Oz*, I've come in contact with folks who have helped and inspired me. Thanks to:

Larry Ramsey, from I.S. 320, whose middle school productions I watched from the audience, wishing I had the guts to be a part of them. Robert A. Levy, Jerry Majzlin, and Janet Lipschultz from John Dewy High School, who introduced me to the joys of theatrical productions. The friends I made doing "what we did for love" and the lessons I've learned have stayed with me all my life. We must never stop funding the arts! *Mango Delight*'s first readers, Maria Perez-Brown and Robin Reid, for their encouragement and assurance that I was hitting the right notes. My writing group members, Jamie Scott, John Meyer, and James Reynolds, who bolstered my confidence with their critique and friendship.

A special thanks to Liz Nealon, who gave me my very first writing job. She has selflessly opened doors for me and has, by example, taught me to be generous, gracious, and humble along the way.

My agent, Kevin O'Connor, and the Charlotte Sheedy Literary Agency for taking a chance on *Mango*. Kevin's guidance, direction, honesty, and insight helped me strengthen the narrative and fill in "blanks" I was not aware of in nascent drafts.

There are scores of people who work tirelessly to make a book and its author look their best. I'd like to thank Irene Vandervoort, Kayla Overbey, Brian Phair, Hanna Otero, Ardi Aslpach, and Sari Lampert of Sterling Publishing. A special thanks to Frank Morrison, an artist I have admired for years, for the wonderful cover illustration.

At the head of this amazing Sterling Publishing team is my editor, Brett Duquette. His patience, insight, and enthusiasm have been invaluable to me. He is the man behind the curtain, the Wizard of this journey to Oz.

From the deepest recesses of my heart, I have to thank my daughter, Jamaya Blue Rhoden-Hyman, for inspiring me to stop complaining about the lack of books with images that look like her on their covers and write one. I wrote *Mango Delight* for her and her rainbow coalition of friends who are hungry to read stories that reflect the new world order of their diverse generation.

To my husband, Ricaldo Ricardo Rhoden, the tornado of love that blew into my life and turned everything all around and upside down and dropped me over the rainbow to a life of love, family, and authenticity. Together, we've crawled out onto the skinny limbs of a rapidly evolving society, where we hold on and thrive against all odds. You and me, babe!

Last, but not least, BIG HUNKS OF LOVE to all of you readers out there. Thank you for taking a chance on Mango and me.